CLONE
RANGERS
D0496816

CLONE RANGERS

Emma Laybourn

Andersen Press • London

First published in 2003 by
Andersen Press Limited,
20 Vauxhall Bridge Road, London SW1V 2SA
www.andersenpress.co.uk

British Library Cataloguing in Publication Data available
ISBN 1 84270 300 5

Typeset by FiSH Books, London WC1
Printed and bound in Great Britain by Mackays of Chatham Ltd., Chatham, Kent

Chapter 1

'Scalpel.'

The blade flashed as the little nurse passed it over.

'Doesn't look good,' the surgeon muttered. 'This leg will have to come off.'

'Oh, no!' The little nurse gazed sorrowfully at the limp figure on the operating table. 'What a shame, especially after he rescued those City children from the fire . . . '

The surgeon shook her head. 'He should have got out of the building faster. At least he'll still have three legs. If we lose the leg, we can save the dog.'

'But he's so badly hurt!' whispered the little nurse.

'Nothing that time won't cure. Get ready to clamp.' The surgeon busied herself with the saw: its remorseless buzz rasped through the operating theatre. 'It'll take time, and money,' she went on, 'but those are Garracker's orders – save the dog, whatever the cost.'

'Garracker?' The little nurse froze for an instant, then glanced around nervously, as if expecting to see him swaggering in with a battalion of bodyguards.

'Garracker,' said the surgeon firmly.

'But why? Why is Garracker so interested in a dog?'

'Not just *any* dog. This is Officer Admiral Benbow of the City Police, and I'm told he's the best undercover agent they've ever had.'

'He won't be going back undercover with three legs,' mourned the nurse.

'There's another thing,' said the surgeon. 'He's *voiced.* One of the few successes. There won't be any more voiced dogs, not until they lift the ban on genetic engineering. More swabs, please.'

The little nurse handed them over, watching the surgeon's deft fingers at work. 'I wonder why so few of the experiments worked,' she wondered aloud.

'It takes more than a voice-box for a dog to speak Human,' said the surgeon gruffly. 'It needs the right palate, jaw, tongue – and most of all, intelligence. No point giving a dog a voice if it has nothing to say.'

'What a lot of trouble, just to make voiced dogs to police the City...'

'They had to,' said the surgeon. 'Human police wouldn't do it any longer – the City got too dangerous. Most of its population are dogs, anyway.'

'And the rest are children. How many are there?' asked the nurse curiously.

The surgeon shrugged. 'Who knows? Who cares? If they choose to live there, how can anyone stop them? It's the police dogs who keep the City under control. So if Garracker tells us to save this dog's life, we do it.' The surgeon bent over the body on the table, cutting, swabbing, sewing.

The nurse gently touched a ragged ear protruding from the oxygen mask.

'Poor Benbow! They said he was going back for the third child when the building collapsed. Are the children he rescued all right?'

'Two are fine,' replied the surgeon. 'Bruises, shock. They'll be out of hospital soon – though goodness knows where they'll go . . . '

'City children? They'll find homes for them, surely?'

'Or a Home . . . They might prefer to return to the City.'

The nurse shuddered, thinking that even an orphanage must be better than the City. 'What about the third child?'

'Badly burnt,' said the surgeon shortly. 'Lost an eye. Scarred for life. There we are.' She dropped the detached leg with a pling into a metal dish.

'Finish the stitches,' she commanded. 'And make it tidy. I've left enough tissue to fit an artificial leg.'

'A *what*?'

'Garracker's orders.' The surgeon handed the needle to the little nurse, who began to stitch carefully, anxious to do a good job. It wouldn't do to displease Garracker . . .

'Finished,' she said ten minutes later, inspecting her own work approvingly. 'Very neat, don't you think?' She turned to see if the surgeon agreed. 'Well! Where's she gone? You'd think she'd stay to see the job done! When it's a hero and all whose leg she's just cut off . . . '

Her voice trailed away, as she looked around for the dish containing Admiral Benbow's leg.

But that had vanished too.

Chapter Two

The little nurse noticed the girl first; her red hair glowed like a bright flame at the end of the ward. The nurse trotted briskly over.

'What do you want? We've got a ward full of very sick dogs here, and it's not visiting time . . .' Then she saw a boy hiding behind the girl. His head was tightly wrapped in bandages. A black patch over one eye gave him a piratical look at odds with his small, thin frame. The other eye peered around anxiously.

'Natty? Is he here?' he whispered.

'He's here, Wilf.' The girl patted his hand reassuringly, and turned to the nurse. 'Please may we see Admiral Benbow – just for one minute?'

The nurse hesitated. She ought to send them packing: but the eye-patch jogged her memory. 'Is your brother one of the children he saved?'

'Wilf? That's right. They were looking for mushrooms in an empty building, when the fire started – I don't know how. Admiral Benbow dragged them out. He'd just gone back for Wilf when the ceiling fell in and trapped them both.'

'Come along, then,' said the nurse, filled with pity. She hurried them towards the bed where the big dog lay.

He was a powerful dog, one part retriever, two parts German Shepherd, and the remaining quarter . . . what?

The nurse couldn't decide. Something swift and shaggy, like a wolf-hound, except that his jaw was too broad, and oddly-shaped. She checked his monitor: heartbeat steady, condition stable. He lay limply on his side, his coat clean and shining, for the nurses sponged and brushed him daily; but his eyes were closed, his breathing soundless.

Wilf stared down at the dog's right foreleg. It ended in a neat, bandaged stump. He put up a hand to touch his eye-patch.

'I lost an eye, he lost a leg,' he murmured.

'He's getting a new one, though,' said the nurse, straightening the sheet. 'A nice, plastic, electronic leg. It'll be almost as good as the real thing.'

Wilf shook his head. 'It won't *be* the real thing.'

'He'll hardly know the difference,' said the nurse, as a shrill yapping started up at the other end of the ward. 'All right, Dodie! I'm coming!' She hurried off to attend to a fretful poodle.

Natty gently pulled Wilf's sleeve. 'Wilf? We've seen him now. There's nothing else we can do.'

Wilf laid his hand upon the dog's warm, rough flank, feeling its slow rise and fall, like the swell of a quiet sea.

'He's looking at me,' he whispered, for the dog's eye had half opened, deep and dark as a well.

'He can't see us, though,' said Natty. Slowly the eye closed again.

'I wish I could do something for him,' said Wilf.

'We will. I promise. But we can't stay here! They'll be missing you soon.'

‘I’m not going back to the ward,’ said Wilf. ‘They’re talking about sending me to a home.’

Natty caught her breath. ‘*What?*’

‘They thought I was asleep,’ said Wilf in a low voice. ‘I heard the doctor say my dressings could come off next week, and asking where I’d be sent. And someone said, “He’s a City child. No family. He’ll have to go to a home.”’

‘A home, or a Home?’

‘I don’t know,’ said Wilf. ‘I don’t want either. *You’re* my home, Natty. You’re my family. I just want to be with you – and Admiral Benbow.’

Natty considered quickly. A good foster home might be the best thing now for Wilf, frail and damaged as he was. But a bad home – or worse still, a Home, an orphanage – would be disastrous. She imagined what Wilf would go through amongst unsympathetic strangers, with his terrible scars and his missing eye.

Wilf was a City boy. Had been since babyhood. But now life in the City wouldn’t be easy for him either.

She made her decision. Wilf should have what he wanted.

‘All right,’ she said. ‘We’ll go before we’re missed. Quickly. *Now*.’

‘Where to?’ Wilf stared.

‘Just come on! Quick!’

He stroked Admiral Benbow one last time, then turned away to follow Natty. Behind him, the dog’s eyes slowly opened, stared blankly at the two departing backs, and closed once more.

Chapter Three

Admiral Benbow lay awkwardly on the couch, his plastic foreleg stretched out stiffly. His nose twitched – the leg still smelt strange, four months after its fitting, and ten months after his old leg had gone. At least he was getting used to its appearance. It didn't give him quite such a heart-jarring shock every time he looked down.

Beyond the alien scent of the leg drifted other, more familiar odours: disinfectant; bathwater, metal-scented from the tank; the comforting promise of reheated gravy for his evening meal. Hospital smells that cocooned him, lulled him, as did the reassuring clank of the approaching trolley and the nurses' chatter.

Benbow turned his head drowsily to the window. His move to the convalescent wing had been a great improvement, for it meant his own room, no more tubes and wires, and a view that stretched right across the Fringes to the dark heart of the City.

His eyes were drawn there now. The City's ragged towers were silhouetted against the sunset. A few sparse dots of light flickered here and there – cooking fires, whose glimmer made the surrounding darkness seem yet darker.

Benbow clambered swiftly down from his couch to nose the window open. The City's smell came riding in on the evening air: smoke and concrete, rats and rottenness, a mixture as harsh as an alarm bell. His heart contracted, tight in his chest. Ten months without the City…

'How are you, Admiral?' Nurse Browning entered, a little round swift bullet of a nurse. She marched briskly to the window and slammed it shut. 'That's better!' she said, with a mock shiver.

'I'm fine, thank you,' said Benbow.

'How's the leg?'

'Fine.' Benbow replied tersely, not because of any difficulty speaking – his voice-box was undamaged – but because his leg was not, in fact, fine. His leg *hurt*.

The stump itself didn't hurt, for the plastic leg fitted comfortably enough. It hurt where his leg *wasn't*. That was why the sight of the plastic gave him such a shock – because he could still feel the vanished leg. Cramps and aches and prickles needled the non-existent skin right down to the absent claws.

'Jolly good,' said Nurse Browning. 'Here's tea.' She slapped the bowl onto the table, twitched at Benbow's blanket, fidgeted with his water, swivelled the ragged bunch of flowers that someone had sent him, and coughed several times.

'You've got a visitor,' she said suddenly. 'I saw him downstairs. But I'm not supposed to tell.'

'Then don't,' said Benbow, folding down his ears. But she darted to his side and whispered in a hurried gust:

'Garracker!' With that, she grabbed the trolley and shot out through the door.

Benbow shook his head free of the word. His eyes

turned back towards the view. Necklaces of buzzing traffic circled the Fringes around the City's edge, stringing outwards to the country, to the houses of the well-to-do in their walled and gated villages. But no traffic entered the City.

How long, Benbow wondered, since the City had fallen into decay? Years before he was born, the shops and offices had starting closing down, moving to new sites in the countryside, clean and vandal-free. The high tower-blocks emptied, slowly at first, then with gathering speed. As flats fell vacant, gangs broke in and smashed them up. The streets filled with broken glass and litter.

Soon no one wanted to live in the City any more. The college and the theatres were boarded up, the hospital closed down, buses stopped running. Gangs roamed the streets, looting and burning. The City Council declared the damage too expensive to repair, shut the Town Hall and moved out.

The police went on strike, refusing to patrol the streets. As rats and disease spread, even the gangs left. Barbed wire went up around the empty City.

But it didn't stay empty. Lost and lonely children, the homeless and the runaways, crept through the wire with their dogs to form new gangs and make new homes in the silent tower-blocks. Theirs was a dangerous life; the burnt-out towers were crumbling year by year. Every so often one collapsed entirely, so that huge grey flowers of dust blossomed from the rubble.

That was when police dogs moved back in. Humans

didn't want to know. Policing the City was a thankless task...

'Miss it, do you?' said a voice. *Not* the nurse's. But even without her warning, Benbow recognised it from Elise's fuzzy radio back at the City Station.

'Garracker,' he said. It came out as a bark. Garracker grinned. His teeth were white and perfect in a lined, tanned, handsome face. He closed the door silently and strolled towards the chair.

'May I sit down?' Carefully adjusting the knife-sharp creases in his trousers, he settled himself opposite Benbow, and crossed his legs. 'I expect you want to get back to work.'

'I doubt if the service will take me back with *this*.' Benbow raised his plastic paw.

'Why not? It's the best leg money can buy,' said Garracker. 'I should know. I bought it.'

'You?' A growl rumbled in Benbow's throat.

'Sure. Who else? Who do you think is paying for this lot?' Garracker waved a careless hand around.

'Dogs' Benevolent Fund, they said.'

'They're not as benevolent as *this*. I've paid for it, Benbow – with a reason.'

Benbow waited.

But Garracker seemed unwilling to go on. He jumped out of the chair and began to prowl around the room, sleek and powerful as a cat, despite the grey that speckled his black hair. Halting by the window, he stared out at the dusk.

'My City,' he said.

Benbow frowned. Garracker was rich; the richest businessman around. If his wealth came from crime – as was rumoured – it had never been proved in court. He had the City Council eating from his hand. But this was the first Benbow had heard of his owning the City.

'My City . . . It's beyond repair.'

'Not necessarily,' said Benbow, pained.

'Beyond repair,' repeated Garracker. He let the blind rattle down, shutting the City out. 'I want to tell you what happened to your leg, Benbow.'

'Beyond repair,' said Benbow wryly.

'But not beyond use,' said Garracker. 'Your leg was . . . used.'

'Used? How?' Benbow's mouth went dry.

'Cloned,' said Garracker.

'You cloned my *leg*?'

'We cloned *you*, you numskull!'

'That's illegal,' said Benbow automatically. 'Has been since 2012, unless you're a government laboratory.' He realised too late that it was not a tactful answer. The man stared at him with eyes as hard as sapphires.

'Don't tell *me* what's legal,' said Garracker, barely opening his mouth. 'We cloned you. Don't ask who did it for me. We didn't need the whole leg, but it was convenient to have so much to work with. We had three successes. Yes. Three nice little clones. Three perfect Benbows.'

Benbow could hardly speak. He felt as though he had just swallowed his dinner, whole, in the tin. '*Why?*'

Garracker swiftly patted his shoulder. 'Because I need you, Admiral! The police force needs you.'

'You don't run the City Police,' objected Benbow.

'I do now. You think the Council can afford to keep them going without my help? You think they want to pay for any of the City's problems? I fund the police, and the Council give me a free hand.' Garracker smiled thinly. 'And you're the best dog we've got.'

'Not with three legs,' said Benbow. The missing limb began to tingle. 'You made three new Benbows. Replacements?'

'They're not designed to replace you, Benbow. How could they?' Garracker's kindly earnestness filled Benbow with distrust. 'You're to work together. They're just pups still – fine young pups – but they need a teacher. A leader. *You*. That's why I paid for all this,' – Garracker swept his arm around again, knocking over the vase of shabby flowers – 'the surgery, the twenty-four-hour care, the leg.'

Benbow was deeply suspicious. His stay in hospital must have been a vast expense, and Garracker was not a man to waste money on good causes.

'I don't understand,' he said bluntly. 'There are other police dogs. Excellent dogs, some of them voiced. Why does the City need three new Benbows?' I certainly don't need them, he thought.

Garracker's eyes flickered. 'You're right, Benbow. Smart dog. There is something I haven't told you.' Smoothly he walked to the door, flung it open to survey the empty corridor, and closed it silently. Definitely cat-like, decided Benbow. No affinity with dogs at all.

'I'm not prepared to tell you here,' said Garracker.

'Come to my office tomorrow morning, nine. Top floor, Prospect Towers.'

Benbow felt no inclination to agree. 'I was assuming I'd retire,' he said.

'You can't.' The man's voice sharpened. 'You're too young. You'll get no pension.'

'There's other work.'

'Who wants a crippled dog?' snarled Garracker. 'You'll end up a flea-bitten stray! And what about your clones? They're no use to me without *you*. No use at all. Might as well be rid of them.' His eyes glittered. 'Be there, Benbow.' Without waiting for an answer, he strode out.

Benbow looked down at his cold, expensive dinner congealing in its bowl. His appetite had gone. Now what? he thought. I could ignore him. Just leave; just disappear.

But there were the clones . . . three pups he didn't want. Did they really exist? If they did, how could he leave them to Garracker's mercy?

Then there was the City, and its children . . .

A memory brushed its wing across his mind. A face white with bandages, a black, patched eye, the other eye wide and pleading . . . Benbow shook his head. Picking up the fallen flowers, he set them back in their vase. Then he pulled up the blind again.

There was the City, waiting for him through all his long sleep. He had thought it must be lost to him forever.

Now Garracker was giving him the chance to return. Of course he would obey Garracker. He had to go back.

Chapter Four

Benbow's new leg was the best walker of the four. The other three were weak from lack of use, but he sensed the plastic leg would never tire.

He did not go straight to Prospect Towers. It was two miles away, thirty minutes through the business zone: the office blocks of mirrored glass and concrete, built by Garracker a safe distance from the City.

But Benbow did not want to go that way. Cold gales blew between the offices, and there were no dogs apart from rushed and edgy errand hounds. So Benbow chose the long way, looping through the Fringes: the bleak estates that encircled the City, just outside the wire.

He plodded through squat ranks of housing blocks adorned with tattered lines of washing. No one lived here if they could afford somewhere better. Shouting children chased each other through playgrounds in which every swing and slide was broken.

Still, thought Benbow, at least these children had homes. Families. This wasn't the City. A pair of dogs came trotting up to sniff a casual welcome in a way that City dogs would seldom do, and did not shy away at the police badge on his collar.

'What's new round here?' Benbow asked in Dog, a combination of barks, head tilts, and tail position. For of course these dogs were not voiced, and while they probably understood Human, it would be impolite to address them in it.

'Oh, nothing,' said the foremost dog, a nervous whippet. 'Nothing new, couple of stolen cars, dog fell off a balcony and broke a leg, had a murder the other day.'

Benbow's ears pricked. 'Murder? Who?'

'Oh, just a man. His dog was all right. A shopkeeper – two men took his money, stabbed him and ran off, into the City.'

'Laughing,' said the second dog, a quiet mongrel.

Benbow nodded. 'They won't laugh long, in there.' A year ago it would have been his job to hunt the murderers down, get them out of the City and into jail. 'Anyone else gone under the wire?'

'A few,' said the quiet dog. 'Three children and a collie. Usual thing – father in prison, mother dead. A couple of runaways last month. Two girls. No dogs.'

'Thanks,' said Benbow. Nothing had changed, then.

'Heard about our monsters?' offered the whippet.

'Monsters?'

'Big machines, black and yellow.' The dog made a get-off-me-wasp gesture. 'By the fence – they've been there months!'

'Will you show me?' asked Benbow.

The two dogs willingly agreed. Leading Benbow through the dingy streets, they scampered over a rubbish tip and wriggled under a tangle of barbed wire. Benbow found himself looking across a wide ribbon of wasteland to the cracked and broken teeth of the City towers.

Nearby, as promised, stood three monsters, caged

behind a tall wire fence: armed and clawed, poised like giant predators. Beneath them dozed two German Shepherd dogs. At Benbow's approach, the guard dogs leapt to their feet and barked terse warnings through the wire.

'Keep off! Get out!'

Benbow raised his head to reveal his badge. 'Whose are these machines?'

'Ours!' 'Off!' 'Go away!' barked the guard dogs.

'What are they for?'

'Don't know!' 'Ours!'

'They're for knocking down buildings,' said the mongrel wisely. 'I've seen 'em do it. Knocked down a house in twenty seconds flat.'

Benbow scrutinised them. There were two huge, clawed earth-movers, and a lanky crane. Then a sudden movement caught his eye. From behind the crane, two small humans scuttled over to the fence and began to climb.

'Are you blind?' barked Benbow at the guard dogs. 'Look! Intruders!'

The dogs spun round, and barking heroically, raced over to the fence. But the intruders had already scrambled too high up the shivering wire for them to reach; they leapt and snarled in vain. Soon the humans were astride the fence, and starting to descend on the outside. They were only children.

'Quick,' said Benbow. 'Intercept!' He loped towards them. His new leg did not run as smoothly as it walked, and he was soon overtaken by the whippet, who yapped nervously at the children. Benbow saw them clearly now: a boy and a girl. The boy jumped down, dashed past the flinching whippet, and ran off with Benbow and the mongrel in pursuit.

At peak fitness, Benbow could outrun any human with ease. But now, to his dismay, he realised that not only was he dreadfully unfit, but his plastic leg slipped and juddered with each stride. The boy was getting away.

'Stop!' yelled Benbow, in Human. For an instant, the boy slowed in surprise.

The instant was enough. Benbow leapt on his back, bringing him down carefully, but firmly, a leg planted on each sprawling limb.

'Name!' he barked. The boy twisted vainly. 'I said *Name*!'

And then the plastic leg collapsed. It snapped out of its socket and sent Benbow lurching sideways. At once the boy writhed out from beneath him and raced away. The mongrel chased him; Benbow couldn't. He tried to run on three legs with the fourth dangling, and had to give up.

He lay down, panting, and watched the girl take a flying leap off the fence. Ponytail streaming, she sprinted past the whippet, who bounded alongside her, yelping, 'Oh, please stop! Please stop!'

'Halt!' barked Benbow. 'You're under arrest!'

The children didn't pause. They ran into the shadows of the City, and were gone. The two dogs gave up the chase and came trotting back to Benbow.

'Sorry,' panted the mongrel, 'I'm not big enough to bring them down. And I'm not following them in *there*.'

'Never mind,' said Benbow. 'You did well. Thank you both.' He was struggling to replace his false leg. At last he thought he'd done it; stood up cautiously. The leg felt fine. Benbow felt terrible.

I got that wrong, he thought. Should have let the boy go, caught the girl instead. Now I've got neither. This isn't going to work. Not just the leg. Brain as well. I'm rusty.

He hobbled to the fence where the German Shepherds waited sheepishly.

'Never smelt 'em!'

'Couldn't see 'em!'

'I wonder what they wanted,' Benbow said. He decided they'd just been mucking around, most likely, looking for something to steal. Though they could hardly steal those vast machines . . .

'Well, at least they didn't get away with anything,' he said. 'Their hands were empty. So I shouldn't worry.'

As Benbow finished speaking, the crane blew up.

Chapter Five

'You're late,' said Garracker.

'A problem with my leg.' Benbow decided against mentioning the explosion. Anyhow, Garracker evidently had other things on his mind. The big man swivelled restlessly in his leather armchair, fidgeting with a gilt-framed picture on his desk, picking it up and laying it down again with a frown.

'Sit,' he said. Benbow sat up on the grey silk carpet, and waited. Garracker leaned forward.

'*Clones*,' he said.

Benbow cocked an ear politely.

'Not yours,' said Garracker. 'Ten years ago – no, eleven now – I decided to have myself cloned.'

Benbow wondered how he should respond. Eleven years ago, cloning had been just as illegal as now. 'Congratulations.'

Garracker nodded. 'I'm not getting any younger,' he said. 'I wanted someone to hand it all on to, to run my business after me. I can see what you're thinking.'

Benbow blinked. He hadn't been thinking anything.

'Why not have a child the usual way?' continued Garracker. 'But then it wouldn't be all mine. Wouldn't be *me*. Might be its mother's: that wouldn't do at all. I wanted to be sure my sons – my clones – would think as I do, act as I do, always. Bound to, aren't they?'

Benbow nodded, doubtfully.

'They made four copies of me,' said Garracker. He sighed. 'In those days, I had more enemies. Word got out. The clones were being raised together, in a nursery. Unwise of me, I suppose – they should have been kept apart. They'd just turned one when they were kidnapped. I was sent a ransom note, by Arkheim – you remember him? No, before your time.'

But Benbow said, 'I remember stories. A bank robber, gangster. Shot dead, wasn't he?'

'Knifed,' said Garracker with certainty. 'I don't like blackmail. I wouldn't pay his ransom. I thought I could outwit him; nearly did – but not quite. He abandoned the babies to the wild dogs in the City. Sent me a body. What was left of it.' Briefly, Garracker closed his eyes.

'It was one of my clones,' he said. 'I assumed the other three were dead as well. Arkheim only outlived them by a week.' The fist on the table was clenched. Then, slowly, it relaxed.

'I put it out of my mind,' said Garracker. 'No use brooding on what's gone. I could have started again with new clones, but . . . ' He shook his head. 'I didn't have the heart.'

Benbow raised an eyebrow.

'In any case,' said Garracker, 'controls on cloning got much tighter after that. The doctor I'd employed had to flee the country. So that was that – till now.'

'And now?'

Garracker stood up, and went to the table by the door. Pouring himself a coffee from a steaming pot, he added a slug of whisky from a cut-glass decanter.

'Coffee?' he asked. 'Beef tea? Or something stronger?'

'Beef tea, please.'

Garracker nodded, poured it from a silver thermos into a china dish, and set it down before Benbow. Benbow lapped cautiously, conscious of the noise, and anxious not to drip on the carpet. He licked his lips and sat back. It was excellent beef tea. He wondered, fleetingly, what the dogs at the City Police Station would be breakfasting on . . . rat, probably, and rust-flavoured water.

Garracker drained his coffee in two gulps, and slammed the cup down.

'I've had a threat,' he said. 'A year ago, *this* came.'

He tossed a letter on the carpet. Holding it flat with his paw, Benbow scanned it carefully, translating the Human symbols into Dog. It was clumsily written, childish . . . but not that childish.

Benbow read:

'I hear you're planning to destroy the City.
If you do, I'll destroy YOU, and blow up Prospect Towers.
Don't try it!
Signed,
THE CITY CHIEFTAIN.'

'Are you planning to destroy the City?' asked Benbow, a strange panic seizing him.

'I *was*. After Arkheim . . . I wanted to flatten it, forget. I've been buying it up, block by block, for years. It's all mine now: I'd just bought the last piece when that letter arrived. I planned to knock the City down and start again.

A new business empire, bigger and better than this one . . . I had architects draw up designs, a mighty forest of steel and glass . . . ' Garracker stared out of the window. 'Oh, I had great plans.'

'Had?'

'That letter stopped me in my tracks.'

Benbow's eyes narrowed. 'It's a serious threat,' he said cautiously. But Garracker waved a dismissive hand.

'It's nothing,' he said. 'I get threats all the time. Small-time crooks, think they're somebody. I determined to track down the sender, naturally, in order to deal with him. He'd been careless: inside the envelope he'd left a single hair.'

'A hair?'

'I had it analysed. They checked its DNA against that of every known criminal in and around the City.'

'And?'

'The hair was mine,' said Garracker. 'I had sent it to myself.'

Benbow followed his gaze through the gleaming window. Across the Fringes, the grey towers of the City faced them, like a broken reflection in dirty water.

'The City Chieftain,' said Garracker quietly. 'A boy after my own heart. One of my clones sent that letter, Benbow: a new Garracker, already building his own empire, sharpening his sword. The threat was bluff, though. He wouldn't have the means to blow up anything bigger than a balloon.'

'I wouldn't be so sure,' said Benbow. Reluctantly, he told Garracker about the exploding crane. Garracker's eyes widened.

'My machines,' he said. 'Waiting for my orders to move in – you *saw* this boy?'

Benbow nodded. Garracker snatched the picture from his desk and thrust it under Benbow's nose.

'Me, aged ten. Is that the boy you saw?'

Benbow studied the photograph. The hair was the right colour, dark like the boy's; the face, with its fierce stare, could be the same – but he wasn't good at recognising human faces. They looked so similar. He identified humans by smell as much as sight.

Surreptitiously, he sniffed the hand that held the photo. Whisky, banknotes, leather... but behind them all lay Garracker's own scent. As Benbow inhaled, memory flooded back: the wriggling boy pinned under him, the leg collapsing. He recognised that scent. Garracker and the boy had smelt the same.

He nodded. 'That's him.'

The knuckles whitened round the picture.

'You had him,' whispered Garracker. 'You had him and you let him go. I *want* him. I want all three of them. I don't believe they're dead. You'll find them, Benbow.'

'Me?'

'Why do you think I had you cloned?' snarled Garracker. 'For your beauty? Why do you think I paid for that damned leg? To see you dance? You and *your* clones, Benbow, will find *mine*. I know they're hidden somewhere in the City. You'll hunt them down and bring them here, to me.'

Chapter Six

Benbow wriggled under the rows of barbed wire that caged the City in. He slunk across the silent wasteland, invisible in the long grass and bitter spires of fireweed. Entering the shadow of the Hopeful Insurance Building, he was back, at last, in the City.

Moss and ivy laced the rotten concrete towers. Weeds waved from rooftops. A sapling grew from a high window ledge, where a seed had rooted: it leaned out like a terrified man about to jump.

Benbow saw no people. But some of the rope-walks were new; perilous woven bridges of rope, chain, and metal tubing, linking tower to tower. Strung across the chasms ten or twelve floors up, they swayed in the sunlight.

Down here below, though, the concrete canyons were as cold as wells. They were choked with the skeletons of rusted cars, long since plundered of seats, wheels, and engines. Some were recent additions – cars crashed by joyriders, then invaded by busy families of rats.

Benbow picked his way carefully, squirming through gaps in the jagged metal. His plastic leg was clumsy, and the leather pouch hanging round his neck, beside his badge, kept snagging.

A shout echoed high above him. Benbow saw a child run along a rope-walk and swing in through a window. A moment later, a row of children's faces appeared in a lower window, while a bunch of dogs came bounding out to meet him.

Four terriers, and two Great Danes. Although big dogs were useful for deterring strangers, they didn't survive easily in the City on their own. Terriers were better at rat-catching, and therefore better fed.

The Great Danes faced Benbow, ready to spring, ears forward in warning.

'You're out of your way!' they barked.

'Just passing through,' said Benbow mildly.

The dogs bared their teeth. 'This is *our* territory. Back! Back!'

'I'm passing through,' said Benbow, watching their legs. When he saw the first dog's muscles tense, he was ready. As it sprang, he stepped aside just enough. The dog tried to twist in mid-air: Benbow grabbed its shoulder in his jaws, over-balanced it, sent it sprawling and leapt on its chest. This time his leg held, and the Great Dane was powerless. Glad to find his strength and skill were not all gone, Benbow raised his head to growl a warning at the second dog, and to reveal the police badge on his collar.

One of the terriers shook his head at the second dog, and approached, eyeing Benbow suspiciously.

'Police? I don't know you.'

'Officer Admiral Benbow. I've been away a long time.'

'I would have remembered that leg.'

'Naturally,' said Benbow. 'The leg's new. But I'm not.'

'There's no trouble here,' said the terrier. 'You don't need to stay.'

'Just passing through,' said Benbow amiably. Standing aside, he let the Great Dane struggle to its feet. It slunk away with a surly backward glance. 'Like I said, I've been away a long time. What's new round here?'

'Nothing.'

'I want to know,' said Benbow gently.

'Nothing changes,' snapped the terrier. 'How should it? We're still cold, wet and hungry. And we still don't like police.'

'Any collapses lately?'

'Nothing serious. Nothing to bother *you*. More fires than usual. Children sick from bad water. Had to take two Out, to hospital. Don't suppose we'll see them again.'

Benbow glanced up at the shabby children peering from the window. Clearing his throat, in Human he called out:

'Children! If you want to leave the City, come to Eagle Square Police Station for assistance.'

The children jeered. A few small stones were pelted down at him.

'No chance!'

'Think we're stupid?'

'We don't need you!'

'Harumph,' said Benbow. Speaking Human loudly was a strain. 'We'll find good homes for you Outside,' he said, adding quickly, 'homes with a small h.'

'Get lost!'

Benbow shrugged. The usual answer. Nodding to the terrier, he strolled away. The dogs watched him, then disappeared into their tower. Benbow scrambled slowly onwards, to the shopping precinct.

Here stood vast department stores devoid of any contents, stripped bare down to the last wire, bolt and hinge. Their walls, scoured by wind and rain, had been redecorated in mould, the floors re-carpeted with ferns and brambles.

Benbow trod carefully, not knowing what new-laid traps might lurk round here. Four times he halted as gangs of dogs and children appeared to confront him. By now they knew his name. News travelled fast in the City – faster than me, thought Benbow ruefully. Three times he had much the same conversation as before.

The fourth gang, though, wore masks.

'That's different,' muttered Benbow. Strange, mottled helmets completely covered the children's heads, with slits for eyes and mouths. Scrawny greyhounds stalked around the gang, who wielded rusty posts like spears.

'Who are you?' said Benbow warily, snuffing in a sour, rubbery odour – the helmets were made of old vinyl flooring. It must be dreadfully smelly inside them.

'Get off our land!' shouted a burly figure, voice muffled. 'Tomahawk? Get rid of him!' Another, taller, child strode forward, gripping its post fiercely.

Benbow looked hard at the speaker. He recognised that roly-poly shape. 'Nile?'

'I'm not Nile. I'm the General!'

'Don't you know me, Nile? It's Benbow. Out of your territory, aren't you? You used to live out east.'

Nile pulled off his helmet, revealing a chubby, sulky

face. 'Thought you were dead, Benbow,' he said. 'Everyone said so.' The taller child shouted,

'We are the Western Warriors! I'm Tomahawk! You're on our land! Get out!' He swung his rusty spear around his head.

'Stow it, Tom,' said Nile heavily. 'This one's police.'

'We don't like police!' hissed Tomahawk, thrusting the spear at Benbow so that it dug into his shoulder.

Benbow didn't move. 'Western Warriors, eh?' he said. 'Any connection with the City Chieftain?'

Tomahawk spat. 'He's our deadly enemy!'

'Why? What's he done?'

'Thief,' growled Nile. 'He stole my territory.'

'Where can I find him?'

'Everywhere. Now go away. See him off, dogs.'

The greyhounds skittered warily up to Benbow.

'Have to chase you away,' muttered one of them apologetically. 'You know what he's like. Have to bark at you now. Sorry.' And they woofed Benbow up the road and out of sight.

Benbow shook his head. Warrior gangs were new to the City; he hoped there weren't any more of them. But he met no one else until he reached Burger Hall, last stop before the Police Station. This had once been Benbow's favourite place to sit, eating a quiet lunch of rat while he waited for a message from the Station. Inside Burger Hall's long-shattered windows, red chairs and tables were still in place; they had confounded looters, being concreted into the floor. Now a rat crouched on Benbow's usual table, nibbling a potato.

A potato? Benbow growled. Where had it got a potato? Potatoes were valuable; a large one was worth three rats . . .

No time to puzzle over it now. He was almost there. He rounded the corner, and, his legs a little shaky, sat down to look.

There it was. Across the square, in a rare patch of sunshine, stood the Police Station. Home. In his past life as an undercover agent, he'd always had to skulk inside in darkness – this was the first time he would ever enter by daylight. In there waited the roaring, coughing stove, his basket with its check blanket, the tired, cheerful banter of Elise and Junior and the other dogs.

But now there would be three new dogs – his clones. It would be like living in a hall of mirrors. Benbow groaned.

The Station door opened, and Tonto the cat hurtled out with an aggrieved yowl. Behind him came a girl with a ragged shock of red hair, carrying an armful of bedding. She began to beat cushions and shake blankets.

A boy followed – her brother, to judge by his mop of identical red hair, even wilder than hers. One eye was oddly black – bruise or dirt? From this distance, Benbow couldn't tell. The boy lugged a tub of soapy water which he tipped into the gutter.

New housekeepers, making the Station ready – for him?

'Hero's return,' muttered Benbow, as a massive volley of barks rang out from the Station. Benbow frowned. He didn't recognise those voices. There were three of them, yet the barks were all the same, overflowing each other like ripples on a beach – three dogs with one voice...

My clones, thought Benbow, his stomach lurching. Do I really sound like *that*? Time to meet them. Gritting his teeth, he plodded up to the faded, peeling Station door.

Chapter Seven

'Admiral Benbow!' cried the red-haired boy. He ran forward, then halted. Benbow saw that the black eye was a leather patch; around it, the skin was raw, pink and stretched. A smell of antiseptic hung around him – a prickly hospital odour.

Benbow frowned, as something tugged at the corner of his mind. He nodded curtly, and went in.

Elise pattered down the hall to meet him. The collie's muzzle was greyer than he remembered; her voice huskier, as it tried to penetrate the frantic barking from upstairs.

'Benbow! At last! Thank goodness! We had a message to say you were coming.'

Benbow saluted his Head of Station. 'Admiral Benbow reporting for duty.'

'Yes, yes. Just go and sort them out! They've only been here a week, and they're driving me crazy!'

Benbow leapt up the stairs three at a time. As he bounded into the dormitory, the barking stopped.

Three dogs stood there, with their front paws in a single dog-basket. Tall dogs, all the same patchy brown, gawky with youth, stiff with surprise.

'*My* basket,' said Benbow. The six paws were lifted out in silence. Benbow stepped into his basket, turned round twice, sniffed the blanket – musty – and lay down.

Only then did he look at them properly. Strangers' faces stared back. Benbow seldom got to see a mirror. Just as well, he thought wryly, if that's what he looked like. Odd set of the jaw. One ear was crooked. The dogs were nearly his height, but skinnier. Made him feel heavy and old.

'Don't you have your own baskets?' he asked gruffly.

'They have blankets,' said Elise, plodding wearily through the door, 'but mostly they just have *arguments*.'

'There'll be no more of that,' said Benbow severely. He felt like his own grandfather. 'Names?'

Elise gave a short, warning cough. 'They were named by their foster homes,' she said. 'Brought up separately, you see; that's half the trouble. This one's Star of Araby.'

Star of Araby looked a fraction taller and leaner than the other two. He stretched his front legs, cocked an ear, and looked down his nose at Benbow.

'I didn't ask to be cloned,' he said. 'I'm not thrilled about being a copy. Especially— '

'Right, next,' said Benbow briskly.

'Huck Finn McCool,' said Elise. 'No, I don't know why either.'

'Don't you ever groom yourself, McCool?' asked Benbow, noting the young dog's matted coat with disapproval.

'Nope. Grooming's for poodles.'

'And police dogs. Get your coat clipped. Next?'

The third dog bounced forward eagerly. 'I'm Daffodil.'

Benbow looked at Elise.

'I'm afraid so,' she said.

'Daffodil anything?'

'No, just Daffodil,' replied his clone, tail wagging at double speed. 'And may I say what a great honour and privilege it is—'

'Yes, right, thanks,' said Benbow. 'We'll take that as said. Araby, I didn't ask to be cloned either. Sit down, all of you.'

They sat, Daffodil most promptly, and Araby last.

'Elise?' Benbow beckoned her beyond the doorway where his clones wouldn't hear. 'Elise,' he said quietly, 'there's something wrong with them. They've got no *smell*!' It made them seem like phantom dogs, not fully real.

Elise smiled. 'They smell all right, Benbow. They smell of *you*. That's why you can't detect it – you can't smell yourself. They each had their own scent when they arrived. Araby smelt of horses, and Daffodil had a definite whiff of shampoo, and McCool of cheese and onion pie. *Home* smells. After a week here, they all smell the same.'

'They're me? You're sure?'

Elise nodded. Benbow took a deep breath. If he had had any doubts before, that killed them. These really were his clones. He whirled back into the room, and barked at them, suddenly angry, though he did not know why.

'Sit up! We've got a job to do.'

'Oh, good!' Daffodil's tail thumped the floor.

'What, already?' said McCool.

'I didn't ask—'

'That's enough,' said Elise, interrupting Araby.

'There's no rush, Benbow. Plenty of time. You've only just got here.' She gently licked his coat to calm him. Benbow realised that he was trembling slightly.

'They gave me a shock too, Benbow,' Elise murmured. 'Disconcerting, I know. Take your time. Have some dinner first.'

'What *is* dinner? Rat?'

She shook her head. 'Those two young humans outside took over the housekeeping a few weeks back. They've been working wonders. They've scrubbed the whole place down, cleaned the stove, stopped the leaks, and we only get rat four times a week now. They've got pork for us today, since it's a special occasion. Heaven knows how – it must have cost them thirty rats!'

'Or ten potatoes,' murmured Benbow thoughtfully. 'In that case, I'll tell you about our assignment over the pork. And then we'll go out on patrol. Been on patrol yet?'

'Not yet, Admiral!' panted Daffodil.

'Nope,' said McCool. Araby said nothing.

'*I* wasn't going to take them,' said Elise.

'Then I will,' decided Benbow. 'I've got visits to pay, and questions to ask. And the first person I want to see is the Recycler.'

Chapter Eight

Benbow prowled restlessly through the Station, trying not to feel like an interloper. Though comfortably full of pork, he was ill at ease.

Was it he who had changed, or the Station? Some of the old dogs, like Junior, were still there; but others, new to Benbow, acted as if they owned the place, making Benbow feel as raw and awkward as his clones. He would have to pretend a confidence he didn't feel, when he took the pups out on patrol.

'Can we come too?'

Benbow glanced at the speaker. It was the red-haired boy; his taut scarred face looked down in confusion. But the girl behind him spoke up boldly.

'You won't remember Wilf, Admiral Benbow, but you rescued him from the fire. And I'm Natty. We came to see you in hospital once.'

'I remember,' said Benbow. Wilf looked up quickly.

'We tried to visit you again,' said Natty, 'only they wouldn't let us in, so we sent some flowers.'

'Indeed,' said Benbow, gazing regretfully at Wilf. He felt responsible for those dreadful scars. He should have got the boy out faster... 'All right,' he said. 'Tag along if you want.'

'Me too,' purred Tonto. The Station cat looked sleeker and better-fed than any of the dogs.

'Oh, no. Why?'

'Old times' sake,' said Tonto silkily. Although he spoke Cat, and Benbow Dog, they understood each other well. 'Just want to see how you do. No offence, Benbow, but you look past it to me. Slow. Clumsy. You know?'

Benbow sighed. There was no point refusing, since Tonto would do what he liked anyway. But it made for a long procession that finally set out on patrol: four dogs – Daffodil proudly carrying Benbow's pouch on his collar – two humans, and a haughty cat. Discretion was impossible, for the clones yapped excitedly as they trotted along.

'This is totally surreal!' said McCool. He gazed skyward at a row of brick gargoyles grinning from the roof of a ruined bank. 'I was brought up in a small town, y'know. This is amazing. Why do humans build things so *big*? And then just leave them when they fall down?'

'Maybe they're saving them for later,' suggested Daffodil. 'Like a bone.' Araby gave him a scornful glance.

'Hey,' said McCool, 'someone's cleared a track through the rubbish down that alley. Wonder where it goes?' He began to lope down the narrow passage.

'Come back!' roared Benbow with furious alarm. McCool halted in surprise.

'Keep your fur on!' he said. 'Only wanted to—'

He never finished his sentence. Benbow sprang on him, hauling him away by the scruff of his neck. Where McCool had been standing, a concrete boulder plunged to the ground and smashed into pieces.

‘Where did that come from?’ he gasped.

‘Third-storey window. You went through the trip-wire,’ said Benbow grimly. ‘Some people round here are very possessive about their territory.’

‘You should have warned us!’ barked Araby indignantly.

‘I’m warning you now,’ retorted Benbow. ‘Rule One: Follow me. Don’t go down strange alleys or into buildings unless I tell you. Rule Two: Look where you’re going. Rule Three: Be polite to everyone – including me, I might add.’

Tonto snickered and sat down to wash.

‘Whose trap is it?’ asked McCool, abashed.

‘Greenspan’s, probably,’ said Benbow. ‘At least, this used to be his territory.’ He looked inquiringly at Natty.

‘Still is,’ she said.

‘Greenspan, Angel, and Nile. Remember those names. They’re the big three – or they were when I was last here. They’ve each got gangs of up to a hundred children, and as many dogs. Though Nile’s gang seems to have shrunk,’ said Benbow, remembering the Warriors. ‘There are dozens of smaller bands too. No one knows how many.’

‘We used to be in Angel’s gang,’ said Natty.

‘But I haven’t seen anyone!’ said Daffodil, mystified.

‘No. The gangs live high up, not at ground level. Too many rats down here. Come on.’ Benbow led them deeper into the City.

No dogs came out to challenge them; no children jeered from windows. His troop was too big, and too obviously police. Police dogs had never been popular with the gangs – although it was the police they came running to, thought Benbow, when fire or collapse threatened their homes.

He felt increasingly unhappy. As an undercover dog, he had been used to travelling in secret. Today, he felt like a tourist guide.

'Cinema,' he said gruffly. The young dogs examined it dutifully. Its floor had collapsed: starlings roosted noisily within.

'Bus station.' The bus stops were still standing, bent at curious angles. The remains of burnt-out buses looked even more depressing than Benbow remembered.

'Museum.' *That* was still intact. Its two-hundred-year-old stones had proved tougher than many newer buildings. Fluted columns paraded across its frontage in an unbroken line.

'Lots of cats round here,' remarked McCool. Cats were rare in the City, because of the dogs; but here, dozens of them twined in and out of the pillars, backs arching at the patrol.

Benbow frowned. 'Know any of them, Tonto?'

'Certainly not!' said Tonto disdainfully. 'They're alley cats.'

Benbow sniffed thoughtfully. Behind the stench of cat lay a dry, rough odour: paper smoke . . . and a hint of burnt rat.

'Ask them what's burning.'

'No offence,' said Tonto, 'but do your own dirty work.' He stalked away.

'I'll ask!' offered Daffodil, but Benbow shook his head.

'You won't understand them. It can wait. It's the Recycler we've really come to see.'

'Who is the Recycler?'

'Been here for ever.'

Wilf piped up. 'She lives in the Colg.'

'The *Colg*?'

'College,' explained Natty. 'The sign's broken. I'm teaching him to read.'

Benbow studied her. 'Who taught *you* to read?'

'My big sister,' said Natty. 'She brought me to the City after my mother went to jail. They were going to send us to a Home, but we ran away, and Angel's gang took us in.'

'Mother *in jail*,' muttered Araby significantly.

'She stole a Christmas hamper,' said Natty, 'because we were hungry.' She stood very straight, and Wilf gently stroked her back.

'She's probably out by now,' said Daffodil anxiously, 'and missing you!'

'I went back once, but she wasn't there. I think they sent her somewhere else. I couldn't find her.' Natty's voice began to sound odd, and Benbow gave Daffodil a warning shake of the tail.

'There's the College gate,' he said. 'Let's go in.'

Inside the iron gates, under the sign '*City Col g* ', a pair of Dobermans barked furiously, not stopping when they saw Benbow's badge.

'I'm closed,' said a voice, and a small, bent woman came into view. She was not much taller than Natty, though much, much older. A pair of hard, bright eyes inspected them.

'Benbow? I heard you were back. All right,' said the Recycler. She slid back bolts, unpadlocked chains, and slowly the gates swung open.

Chapter Nine

The Dobermans retreated reluctantly to let them enter the Recycler's yard. Once a car park, it was now crammed with planks, poles, tyres, tubes, pipes and bricks, all piled into mountains. Between the mountains rose smaller hills of plastic trays, coils of rope, wire netting; and a miniature forest of upturned chair legs.

'Who buys all this stuff?' asked Araby, amazed.

'People. Dogs. There's more inside.' Benbow nodded at the broken shell of the College building.

'This place is a health hazard,' whispered Daffodil. 'Have you seen the *rats*?'

'The whole City is a health hazard,' said Benbow wearily. The Recycler had disappeared behind a mound of radiators and was untying a tangle of wire with deft hands. Her quick, decided movements reminded Benbow of a robin. She didn't pause as he addressed her.

'What's the going rate for a potato?'

'Two and a half rats,' said the Recycler. 'But the price is coming down. Did you want some? I can get them.'

'Where from?'

'That would be telling.'

'What about paper?'

'Expensive,' said the Recycler, shaking her head. 'Has to be imported from Outside.'

Benbow called Daffodil over, and removed

Garracker's letter from the pouch. He held it out, face down. 'What about this sort?'

She gave it an indifferent glance. 'Yes, I stock that. New leg, Benbow?'

'Newish. Are you sure about the paper? Take a good look.'

She sighed, took it and turned it over. Benbow saw her face stiffen. Smelt alarm.

'You can't read that!' yelped Daffodil. 'It's classified! Isn't it classified, Benbow? She's reading it! Can I arrest her? Please?'

'Not now, Daffodil.'

'But I'm dying to arrest someone!'

'Not this someone,' said Benbow. 'You know who wrote that letter, don't you, Recycler?'

'No. The message . . . startled me, that's all.'

'Why? It's addressed to Garracker. You don't care about Garracker. But perhaps you know the City Chieftain?'

'Don't know anyone of that name.' The Recycler began to walk away. Araby sprinted into her path, teeth bared, growling.

'Cut it out, Araby,' said Benbow. 'All right, Recycler. Forget the letter. But you do sell paper. A lot?'

'Not much.'

'Sell any for fuel, to burn?'

She looked startled. 'Of course not! That's wasteful. If you want fuel, I've got coal.'

'What about matches?'

'They're rationed, since I had a load stolen.'

'Who by?'

'How should I know?' She glared at him.

'Never mind. Just put the letter back in Daffodil's bag, please.'

The Recycler obeyed, looking hard at Daffodil and Araby. 'Your sons, Benbow? I didn't know you had children.'

'Close relatives. There's a third one somewhere.' Benbow glanced around for McCool, who was nowhere to be seen. Wilf and Natty were playing on a heap of tyres close to the College building. Natty was trying to encourage Wilf to climb the black pile.

'Look, they're bouncy! You can't hurt yourself!' she cried, bumping down the heap to demonstrate. Wilf began to clamber slowly up, teeth gritted in painful determination.

Benbow turned back to the Recycler. 'Got any children at the moment?'

'Two girls – Helga and Tate. They're out on an errand.' She frowned at the tyres. 'I can't take any more on.'

'That's all right,' said Benbow. 'Those two already have a home.' He eased his artificial leg. 'Mind if I sit down?'

'Does it hurt?'

'Sometimes,' agreed Benbow, wincing bravely. 'Could I have a bowl of water, please?' The Recycler hurried inside the College.

'I'm sorry, Admiral!' said Daffodil, sounding worried. 'I didn't know your leg was hurting! You should have said. Shall we go back to the Station? We'd better go. I'll call—'

'No!' snapped Benbow. The Recycler was returning with a bowl, which she laid before Benbow. As he drank, she fingered his plastic leg.

'Nice piece of work.'

'Yes. You can't buy it.'

'Battery-driven? If you need batteries, I can get them. I'll exchange for any currency except rat.'

'Tinned dog-food?'

'Certainly,' said the Recycler.

Benbow shifted his leg and sipped his water. 'So how are all your children doing?'

'Well, now.' She counted on her fingers. 'Leo and Clifton are working for Greenspan, and Sid's with Nile. Mary and Anneth are in a small gang over west now. Carlo fell off a rope-walk, had to be taken Out to hospital, never came back. Jessie, Ken and Astor—'

'Hang on!' barked Araby. 'How many children has she got? Humans don't have litters, do they?'

Benbow closed his eyes.

'They're not *mine*,' said the Recycler. 'I adopt. A child or two at a time, for a year or two at a time. Sometimes *they* adopt *me*. They help around the yard.'

'I see,' grunted Araby. 'Slave labour!'

'Araby,' said Benbow quietly, 'please go away, find McCool, and tell him to meet us at the gate. Take your time.' He shrugged apologetically at the Recycler. 'You were saying. Jessie, Ken and Astor...?'

'All grown up. Gone Outside.'

'That's a lot of children, over the years.'

'Thirteen, including the latest pair,' said the Recycler

with a touch of pride. She almost smiled.

'They've all survived?'

The smile went out abruptly, leaving her face bleak. 'All but Zola. Died in a fire five months ago. I'd only had her a few weeks. Clever girl. Quiet.'

'Another fire? I didn't hear about that one.'

'Been a lot of fires this year,' said the Recycler, sounding tired.

'Why is that?'

'I don't know. But the dogs keep watch. No one's going to burn *my* yard.'

'Is it a fire-starter, then?' asked Benbow, alarmed.

'How should I know? Had enough water? I've got things to do.' She snatched up the bowl, sharp as an angry sparrow.

'Thanks, Recycler.' Benbow lumbered to his feet. 'See you around. Come along, Daffodil.' Once out of earshot, he asked Daffodil, 'Well? What do you think?'

'I don't know,' said Daffodil anxiously. 'I thought only children lived in the City – but she's *old*.'

'She's the only adult allowed to stay. If any others come in, the gangs kick them out. They tolerate the Recycler because she's always been here, and she's useful.'

'She seems nice.'

'*Nice*?' Benbow considered. 'No. Not *nice*. But she's on the right side.'

'Who's on the wrong side, Admiral?'

'Fire,' said Benbow. 'Famine. Cold. Illness. Loneliness and Fear.'

Daffodil blinked. 'What about the City Chieftain, Admiral?'

'Ah! She knows who he is.'

'Does she?' Daffodil stopped dead. 'Then can't I go back and arrest her, Admiral? *Please*?'

'No. McCool! Araby!' The other dogs sauntered over.

'Admiral? Why do you think she knows?'

'When she saw the letter,' said Benbow, 'it wasn't the contents that shook her. She froze before she'd time to read it. She recognised the handwriting.'

'So?' growled Araby.

'So she knew the writer, very well. In fact, she probably taught him to write. Which means it was one of her own children.'

'But she told us all about them,' protested Daffodil.

'She told us about *twelve* of them,' corrected Benbow. 'But there were thirteen. If we can just discover the name of the thirteenth, the one she didn't mention—'

'Dowie,' said McCool.

Benbow gaped at him.

'I talked to her dogs,' said McCool. 'Do you know, she calls them Dog One and Dog Two? Looks after them well, though. We were chatting about food, and they said they used to live mostly on rat, but now they get real meat, because a boy who once lived here has hit the big time and sends them pork. He's taken over from Nile, they said, and now he's one of the big three: Greenspan, Angel and Dowie.'

'Dowie,' repeated Benbow. 'Good work, McCool. Now, if we can just discover where to find Dowie—'

'I know.' That was Natty.

'You know Dowie?' asked Benbow in a kind of despair.

'No,' said Natty. 'But there's only one place in the City that sells pork.'

'Where?'

'The police aren't meant to know,' said Natty doubtfully. 'The gangs wouldn't like it.'

'It's all right to tell *him*.' Wilf looked trustingly at Benbow. 'We bought our pork at the Town Hall.'

'How much did it cost?'

'Twenty-five rats,' said Wilf proudly. 'I caught them all myself.'

'My word,' said Benbow. He wondered whether to feel put out at having his detection done for him, or worried about his slowness; then decided to just be pleased instead. 'Excellent,' he announced. 'Well done, everybody. We've got what we came for. Let's move on out.'

Chapter Ten

'Back to the Station,' said Benbow. The pups whined with disappointment.

'We haven't seen anything yet!'

'I thought you'd show us the whole City, Admiral!'

'Interesting smell down *that* street,' said McCool, and before Benbow could stop him he was lolloping away. Araby and Daffodil dashed after him, yapping enthusiastically.

'Wait!' barked Benbow. 'Slow down!' But he knew the dogs were full of energy that they needed to expend somehow. They leapt over the litter of the streets, barking at rats, revelling in the chance to run.

'I suppose it won't hurt,' muttered Benbow, as he plodded behind with the children. Suddenly the clones halted. A volley of identical barks echoed down the street.

Benbow felt his hackles rising. Interesting smell? McCool was right. *Very* interesting. It was a smell that made a part of Benbow – the wild, ancient part – awaken eagerly, while his civilised self winced and thought, '*Uh-oh . . .*'

'Stay back!' he ordered the children sharply, spurring himself into a run. The clones stood by an alley lined with broken fire-escapes, and cluttered with mangled cars half-hidden under weeds.

Something else was there, half-hidden, too.

Two bodies lay sprawled on the ground. Not dogs, not children: men. They had been dead for several days. Glancing up, Benbow saw the broken rope of the snare that had caught one; the other had probably run forward to free him, hit the tripwire, and fallen under an avalanche of concrete . . .

A few soggy banknotes lay on the ground. Benbow recalled the mongrel he'd met in the Fringes; the tale of the murdered shopkeeper. *Two men, escaped into the City . . .* and now they would never come out.

'We've got to help them!' yelped Daffodil, starting to run towards the men.

'They're dead,' said Benbow. 'Don't go near! Come back, Daffodil! There'll be another—'

There was a quiet click and an echoing clang. Benbow felt sick. Daffodil looked down blankly.

'Something's got me,' he said in surprise. A set of jagged metal teeth had snapped around his leg like a hungry crocodile's jaws.

'Mantraps,' shouted Benbow furiously. 'Didn't I tell you to be careful? Didn't I tell you not to go down any alleys?' He felt weak with fear and anger, imagining a three-legged Daffodil. It mustn't happen.

'Ow,' moaned Daffodil. 'It's hurting. Help me, Admiral! Oh, I'm sorry! Get me out, please!' He turned up his head and began to howl.

'Stop yowling!' cried Araby fiercely. 'Don't be such a baby!'

'All right,' said Benbow. 'No need to shout.' Hearing the anger in Araby's voice, he realised how he must sound himself. Daffodil was becoming more distressed. Benbow took a deep breath. 'Don't worry, Daffodil! We'll get you out.'

He studied the ground warily. He could see another tripwire, but was that the last? He began to pick a careful path towards Daffodil.

'Natty – follow me!' He would need human fingers to unlock the trap. 'Don't worry, Daffodil,' he said gently, as he approached the whimpering dog, and forced himself to look at his leg.

It wasn't as bad as he feared. The teeth of the trap were wide, and Daffodil's leg was slender. Although the skin was gashed, the bone shouldn't be broken.

Natty tugged at the trap's jaws. 'Can't get it open,' she panted. 'I need a lever.'

'Oh, please hurry!' moaned Daffodil, trembling all over.

'I'm trying!'

'Try this,' said a voice above her. A boy leapt down the fire escape, jumping over gaps in its rusty stairs. He thrust out an iron bar; then, seeing Benbow, halted. 'Police?' he said uncertainly.

'We're friends!' cried Natty.

The boy frowned. 'I know you! Weren't you in Angel's gang?'

'Yes. Give us that bar!'

'*I'm* in Angel's gang now.' The boy put two fingers to his mouth and whistled. More feet clattered on the fire escape.

'Who's caught?'

Benbow knew that voice. Looking up, he saw a small

figure topped with a cloud of fine hair, and his heart lifted gladly.

'Hello, Angel,' he said.

'*Benbow!*' she cried. 'And Natty! What are you doing here? No, don't tell me now – let's get that dog free first.' She ran lightly down the steps. Together they prised open the creaking mantrap, until it released Daffodil's leg.

'Your trap?' asked Benbow gruffly.

'No. This isn't my territory, Benbow. We came over the rope-walks to see what all the barking was about. The trap is probably Dowie's, and meant for Outsiders. Only an Outsider would be silly enough to come down here.' She looked askance at the bodies. 'Can you get rid of them, Benbow?'

'I'll see to it,' he promised. He gave her hand a quick, inconspicuous lick, and Angel smiled.

'My leg hurts,' said Daffodil faintly.

Angel gazed at him. 'He's very like you, Benbow! So are those two others.'

'Same breed,' said Benbow, not wishing to elaborate. He was not sure if Garracker wanted the cloning kept secret.

'Strange. Really very like...' Angel sounded suspicious.

'Daffodil, can you walk?' asked Benbow.

'I think so.'

'This way, then – carefully! Don't step anywhere till I tell you.' Under Benbow's instructions, Daffodil slowly limped back to the road.

'My base is two blocks further down,' said Angel. 'We can't carry you, though.'

'I'll walk,' said Daffodil feebly, and walk he did, limping and moaning gently until Araby told him in a rough undertone to shut up.

Angel led them to a weather-beaten office block. In the hall, children and spaniels huddled around an ancient stove. Daffodil collapsed just inside the door, panting heavily, and Angel ordered water and cloths to clean his wound. McCool galloped upstairs, checking the layout.

'Lots of dormitories,' he reported back to Benbow. 'Cold, but tidy. Folded blankets, clean water in buckets. Looks all right.'

'I know. Angel's a good leader.'

'How's Daff?'

Angel, winding a bandage round the stricken leg, glanced up.

'It looks worse than it is,' she said. 'But I've got no antiseptic.'

'I've got Wilf's ointment back at the Station,' said Natty, 'and we've loads of spare bandages, haven't we, Wilf?'

'All my old ones.'

'How are you now, Wilf?' asked Angel, looking at him compassionately.

'Fine,' said Wilf with determination. 'I like it at the Station, with all the dogs.'

'And what brings all these police dogs over this way?'

'We're searching for Dowie,' said Benbow. 'Do you know him?'

Angel went quite still, looking from Wilf to Benbow. 'Who wants him?'

'Garracker.'

'Ah.' Angel let out a breath. 'Doesn't surprise me. Dowie's been throwing his weight around. I suppose he's annoyed Garracker?'

'Garracker doesn't mean him any harm,' said Benbow carefully. 'He just wants to... talk. Where does Dowie live?'

'Town Hall.'

'He *lives* there?'

'He owns it. He's moved in, just like Lord Mayor, with all the trappings.' Angel sounded amused. 'It's a lot grander than this place!'

'Nothing wrong with this place,' said Benbow. 'But if you ever want to try life Outside—' He knew it was pointless to ask, but that was his job.

'Yes, yes, I know.' Smiling, Angel patted Daffodil's leg. 'That'll do till you get home,' she told him. 'You've escaped lightly! It's lucky you're thinner than Benbow.'

'But I'm not!' burst out Daffodil. 'I'm *exactly* like the Admiral!'

Angel laughed. 'You look like a younger version of him, but you can't be exactly alike, you know.'

'I can! I've got to be!'

'Why?' asked Angel curiously.

'Because I'm his clone! We all are!'

Angel let Daffodil's leg fall. 'Clones?' she said, in an odd voice. She stood up and wiped her hands. 'I knew there was something wrong. Cloned police. Whatever next?' She stared at the dogs in disbelief.

'We didn't ask to be cloned,' said Araby harshly.

'It's unnatural. I'm not sure it should be allowed.'

'It isn't,' said Benbow.

Angel stared at Daffodil as if he were an alien. 'You weren't born. You were *made*, in a laboratory.'

'Only to start with,' said McCool. 'I think we were born too, y'know. Anyway, so what?'

'That's monstrous,' said Angel. 'If you mess around with nature, you make monsters. How could you, Benbow? How could you let them?' She looked down at Daffodil with a cold, appalled glare. 'Get up, clone. You can walk.' Daffodil stood up, tail drooping miserably. 'Get out of here. Go back to the Station. Go on, Benbow. What are you waiting for?'

'The cloning wasn't his idea—' began Araby indignantly, but Benbow nudged him.

'Leave it. Time we went.'

'Natty? Wilf? You still have a home here,' Angel said.

'No, thanks,' said Wilf. 'I told you, I'm happy at the Station.'

'I hope they're not going to clone every dog there,' said Angel icily.

'I'm the only one,' said Benbow. 'Goodbye, Angel. Thank you.'

He left with head and tail upright, although he felt wretched. He wondered why one human's disapproval should make him so unhappy. Doggie instinct, he told himself fiercely, to be severely quashed. Police dogs couldn't afford soft-hearted Doggie instincts.

But as Benbow walked stiffly away, he longed for a hand to stroke his fur, and scratch him gently between his ragged ears.

Chapter Eleven

Next morning, a chill lay over the City. Mist curled in cold ribbons around the Police Station, making the dogs shiver as they emerged.

'Where to, Admiral?'

'The Town Hall, to find Dowie.'

'Oh, good! Can I arrest him, please?'

'*No*, Daffodil,' said Benbow patiently. 'We're just going to buy some pork. But first we need currency. *Rats*. Rat-catching time, everyone!'

'I've never met a rat,' said Daffodil anxiously, dangling his bandaged paw.

'Where I was raised, the stables were full of rats,' drawled Araby. 'They're hardly difficult to kill.'

'Then you can show us how it's done.'

'Oh, no,' said Araby coolly. 'I'll leave that to you. *You're* the expert.'

'Come on, then,' said Benbow glumly. He enjoyed catching rats even less than he enjoyed eating them. 'Round to the tip.'

Behind the Station festered a rubbish tip carefully nurtured by the police dogs, for it provided much of their food supply. Its rotting slopes were tunnelled like a warren, and swarmed with sleek brown rats.

To Benbow's dismay, Elise, Junior and the other Station dogs came out to watch. Even Tonto sauntered over.

'Dear me,' he said. 'Are you sure you're up to this, Benbow?' Benbow, who wasn't sure at all, swore under his breath. He would have to get this right.

He eyed the darting rats until he spotted an unwary one, then pounced. To his relief, he caught it neatly and managed to kill it before it could slither away.

'Back of the neck,' he told the younger dogs, trying not to pant. 'You try.' He sat up to watch them. Junior joined in the hunt, while the other Station dogs barked encouragement, but Elise lay down beside Benbow.

'I'm too old for rat-catching,' she murmured.

'Nonsense!' said Benbow with a worried glance; but he'd noticed that Elise looked older and wearier than he remembered. What would happen when she retired? He couldn't imagine the Station without her in charge. Perhaps Junior could take over?

He watched Junior, a leggy lurcher, dispatch three rats with difficulty. Though enthusiastic, he was too clumsy to be good at this job. Nearby, Daffodil darted frantically on three legs, torn between fear of the rats and his avid desire to catch one. McCool lolloped after a couple, caught them as if by accident, then lost interest and began to nose after a trail of his own.

By now they had another audience – of children, who leaned, cheering, from the upper floors of Burger Hall. Benbow barked a greeting in return. Then he noticed a less welcome sight. A gang in battered, smelly helmets were coming across the Square to watch the dogs. The Western Warriors . . . Benbow sighed.

'I don't like them either,' said Elise quietly. 'We don't

need fighting gangs in the City.'

'People have always squabbled over territory...'

'That's different. Nobody gets hurt, not badly, anyway. But this lot are looking for a fight.'

Benbow stood up, ready to confront the Warriors. But it seemed they had only come to jeer.

'Got nothing better to fight than rats?' shouted the tallest. Benbow recognised Tomahawk's voice.

'Rats is all they can manage! Can't catch anything bigger!' mocked the fattest.

'Come and help us, Nile!' said Benbow. Nile shook his head, backing away.

But Tomahawk, yelling, 'Watch a real fighter at work!' leapt onto the tip, pounced swiftly on a rat, and caught it bare-handed. Stunning it smartly on the ground, he tossed it to Benbow.

'Better'n any dog,' he said. 'At *anything*.' He swaggered back to the gang, and they strolled away, laughing.

'Show-offs,' growled Junior. 'Got no time for that lot. See Araby? He's good.'

Benbow had almost hoped that Araby would fail to catch any rats, thinking it might teach him a lesson in humility. But Araby, eyes half-closed, killed rats with grim efficiency. His only rival was Tonto, who caught six very quickly, and then sat down to wash.

'Too easy,' yawned the cat. 'No offence. I'm sure you're all doing your poor best.' Since the remaining rats had now burrowed into the depths of the heap, where only Tonto could follow, Benbow called a halt.

'Seven,' panted Araby, coughing in disgust. 'I hate rats.'

'Two,' called McCool.

'None.' Daffodil's tail wilted. 'Perhaps it'll be easier when my leg's better.'

'Four!' Wilf displayed them proudly, two limp bodies in each hand. 'I snared them! I've got traps all round the Station.'

'His own design,' said Natty. 'They work really well.'

Benbow looked at Wilf with new respect. 'Good hunting, Wilf!' On an affectionate impulse, he leaned over and licked the boy's bright hair.

'*Don't!*' Wilf shrank away, hands on his head.

'Sorry,' said Benbow, berating himself inwardly for letting the Doggie instinct break out again. He lowered his voice to a rumble. 'Right – let's load these up and head for the Town Hall.'

Daffodil's tail wagged. 'On the way, Admiral, will you tell us all about your greatest arrests?'

'Oh, what bliss,' muttered Araby.

Junior winked at Benbow. 'Wonder where he gets that sarcastic streak from? Must be your fault, Benbow.'

'Naturally,' said Benbow.

The children piled the corpses onto a trolley, and Wilf began to haul it down the street. Natty tried to help, but to her obvious distress was pushed away. Benbow said quietly to her,

'Your brother can manage by himself, you know.'

'He's— ' Natty paused. 'He's not very old.'

'How old is he?'

'About ten. Ten,' said Natty. 'He's changed since the accident – he's quieter. Things worry him. He needs to know I'm close.'

'Not *too* close!' said Benbow. 'Wilf has to do some things on his own. You can't always protect him, Natty.'

At last the spires and great dome of the Town Hall came into sight. Pigeons fluttered from its roof, wings clapping, but none settled on the ground; for pigeons made good eating, and had grown wise.

'Whoa!' said Benbow. In front of the Town Hall, by a dry fountain, sat a boy and a dog – lookouts, he guessed. Sure enough, when a girl came scurrying over from Princess Street, she paused until they nodded at her, and then ran up the broad steps into the Town Hall. Two boys followed from the opposite direction; then two more. Soon Benbow had counted ten children and six dogs entering the Town Hall. By City standards, sixteen was a crowd.

'Remember the plan, everyone?' he growled. 'Wilf will go in with McCool, since he looks the least like a police dog.' McCool grinned. He still hadn't had his coat trimmed, and was scruffier than ever. 'Araby, go round the back and check for other exits. Daffodil: wait here with Natty. Any sign of trouble, just howl.'

'Will you go in and arrest people?' asked Daffodil.

'Not if I can help it,' said Benbow. 'Wilf and McCool will keep the meat-seller busy, so he can't run away when he sees my badge. I'll demand to inspect his trading licence and make a few threats. If I kick up enough fuss, he'll tell me where Dowie is.'

Araby's lip curled. 'Is this what being a police dog is about?'

'Yes,' said Benbow. 'Off you go, Wilf.'

Wilf and McCool ascended the Town Hall steps, watched by the lookouts. Benbow, pausing to give them a head start, snuffed curiously at an unknown smell in the air: a strong, green, sickly-sweet smell that he couldn't identify, but that grew stronger as he approached the Town Hall.

The boy at the fountain stared at Benbow's leg, then whistled shrilly. Quickening his pace, Benbow galloped up the steps and inside.

He couldn't believe his eyes.

It was a *market*. Dozens of stalls spread across the marble floor of the great hall, with dogs and children milling around them.

There wasn't just pork for sale; there were pigeons, and pigeon eggs. And potatoes. And mushrooms. And turnips. Benbow had never seen so much fresh food in the City before: most of the inhabitants lived on tins, pilfered from Outside, along with the occasional stale loaf and box of cereal . . . and of course, rat. There were no rats for sale here.

He saw Wilf haggling with a gangly boy at the meat stall, while McCool snuffled at the meat to hold the boy's attention. But across the hall, two burly mastiffs and a small bull terrier were marching purposefully towards Benbow. He shook his police badge free and swiftly shouldered his way to the meat stall.

'I demand to see—'

A loud crackling noise broke across his words. Benbow froze. It sounded like a handful of pebbles clattering on the marble floor – but it had come from the *ceiling*.

The market fell quiet, as everyone looked around in bewilderment. The bull terrier growled uneasily. There was another ear-splitting crackle, like the first clap of thunder before the deeper boom. Swift and jagged as black lightning, a thin line ran across the stained plaster ceiling above Benbow's head as if drawn by an invisible pen.

Benbow drew a horrified breath, and barked as loudly as he could:

'OUT! OUT! EVERYBODY OUT!'

The black line in the ceiling widened. Flakes of plaster began to fall from it like snow. Children and dogs tripped over each other as they charged for the exit. The gangly boy tried to bundle up his meat, until Benbow sprang at him, teeth ripping his jacket.

'Leave it! Get out *now*!' He saw Wilf standing stock-still, gazing up with fascination. Then McCool lunged at Wilf and barged him towards the door.

'*Out! Out!*' Benbow raced across the hall, herding panicky children, as the strange, hard snow fell all around them. The plaster shower thickened to a flurry – then became a blizzard. A moment later, it was an avalanche.

Huge chunks of plaster tore away from the ceiling and smashed into the floor. A lump hit the bull terrier, knocking it senseless, and Benbow dashed over to grab it by the scruff of its muscular neck. As he dragged the dog across the plaster-strewn floor, black specks began to fall amongst the white. Benbow smelt the dark, raw, living smell of earth, and the cold tang of potatoes.

And then something leapt on his back. For a bewildered moment he thought another dog had pinned him down – but his attacker was bigger than any dog. It was as heavy and smothering as a dozen wet blankets. It was *earth*.

Benbow sprawled helplessly across the bull terrier, nose between paws, trying to keep an air-space open. He was weighed down by a cold, black quilt of earth, enclosing, cradling, crushing him. More soil rained down with a sound like the patter of soft feet in the dark.

Benbow had a terrible feeling that he had been here before. His mind flew back ten months to that dreadful day: the children's screams, the crash of the girder falling, the agony of his trapped leg, the greedy flames licking closer…

His heart thumped in panic. He tried to paw his way out, but could not move. Earth hugged him tight with clammy arms. He was buried alive.

Chapter Twelve

Benbow lay motionless, protecting the pocket of air around his nose. A steady trickle of soil was running in to fill it.

He heard muffled sounds above. Rescuers? Would they reach him in time? The air-pocket was getting smaller, and he had to share it with the unconscious bull terrier.

The soil shifted. Benbow's heartbeats pounded through his head. Then, at last, came the unmistakable scrape of a spade.

Benbow tried to call out, got a mouthful of earth, and forced himself to be still. His lungs ached tightly. As spades rasped above him, his head spun, and lights flashed inside his eyelids. Despite himself, he began to heave and gasp.

A blade scraped his back, and the weight of soil lifted. Hands rummaged for his coat, grasped it and pulled him free into the light and air.

Benbow took great shuddering breaths, drinking air in. He collapsed onto his side, and found himself staring eye to eye at a potato. Slowly his dizziness passed, leaving him trembling with remembered fear.

A rough tongue licked his neck. Benbow rolled an eye upward and saw Daffodil: or was it Araby?

'Where's McCool?' he whispered. 'Wilf?'

'They're fine, Admiral. McCool got Wilf out.'

'Another dog buried with me,' murmured Benbow.

'They're digging her out now.'

Benbow felt as feeble as a newborn pup. Daffodil's tongue licked him consolingly. Nearby, children floundered in the soil, attacking it with hands and spades. Benbow recognised a pony-tailed girl: the one who'd climbed the fence before the crane exploded...

She threw down her spade and pulled at a leg protruding from the soil. The gangly meat-seller emerged in a shower of earth, lay still for a minute, then twitched back into coughing life.

Benbow forced himself to roll over and get to his feet. His plastic leg had slipped, and he spent some time adjusting it, willing his shaky body to calm itself. Araby was glowering at him from the door, cold and angry.

A sudden hush fell over the crowd, and Benbow turned to see the cause.

It was the boy who had blown up the crane.

It was *Garracker*.

A little Garracker, moving with the same assured swagger, while the crowd stepped back respectfully. Natty, looking terrified, clung to Wilf.

'Dowie,' rasped Benbow. 'Police.' He raised his head stiffly to reveal his badge.

Dowie showed no interest. 'Where's Trugg?' he demanded. The bull terrier snuffled over to him, sneezing, and Dowie picked her up. 'All right, Trugg? Good girl! Anyone else under there, Camilla?'

'Don't think so,' answered the pony-tailed girl.

'Where are the lookouts? How many people came in? Count everyone here, make sure the numbers match.' He put Trugg down. 'We'll need sacks. Clear all this soil out, put it in the fountain. But not the potatoes: bag them up, and take them to the Council Chamber. Everyone all right? Nobody hurt?' He gazed around enquiringly, and paused at Wilf.

'They're *old* scars,' said Natty fiercely. 'He's fine. Come on, Wilf, we'll help shovel.' She picked up a spade.

Turning to Benbow, Dowie held up his hands. 'All right, Officer – I agree it wasn't such a good idea, growing potatoes upstairs. It did solve the rat problem, though. And it's legal. Not illegal, anyway. So what are you doing here?'

He spoke calmly, but there was steel in his voice. Benbow knew that he had been recognised. That dratted leg again . . .

'I want to talk in private,' he said huskily. His throat was sore.

Dowie scowled. 'If it's about a certain explosion – you can't prove anything.'

'It's not.'

'Benbow just saved Trugg's life,' said McCool, with a friendly sniff at the bull terrier, who drew back affronted.

Dowie nodded slowly. 'All right,' he said. 'We'll talk upstairs.'

'Upstairs?' Benbow glanced at the huge hole in the rotten ceiling. Through it he could see another, loftier ceiling and wondered if that was equally rotten.

'Don't worry,' said Dowie. 'The potato crop was only

on the first floor. And the pigs are all in the basement, so *they're* not going anywhere.'

He headed for the stairs. As Benbow moved, the three clones followed him automatically, like pins drawn after a magnet. Dowie stopped and stared at them. 'What *is* this?'

'They're part of what I need to tell you,' said Benbow.

Dowie raised an eyebrow, but continued without comment up the grand staircase. Its heavy banisters were freshly polished; the faded carpet had been neatly patched. The walls were hung with portraits of long-forgotten mayors, their paint peeling, though the gilded frames looked newly scrubbed.

'Found all this stuff stowed in the basement,' said Dowie. 'I think it gives the place some style, don't you agree?'

Benbow did not have enough breath to answer. Three floors up, he had to stop and rest.

'For goodness' sake,' muttered Araby impatiently.

'Are you all right, Admiral?'

Benbow nodded. He felt faint, and his paw throbbed. But he mustn't show weakness. He forced himself on, until at last they stood in a small, circular, sunlit room: they were inside the dome at the top of the Town Hall.

Dowie leant against an over-sized desk, with Trugg at his feet. Folding his arms, he frowned at Benbow. 'Well, Officer? What's all this about?'

Benbow fished the letter from Daffodil's pouch. 'You sent this to Garracker.' He could hear himself wheezing like an old dog. 'He told us to find you. Don't worry! He means you no harm.'

Dowie spread his hands innocently. 'I was younger when I wrote that letter – a bit wild. I'm doing things the sensible way now.'

'Like blowing up that crane?' enquired McCool.

'That was Camilla, my explosives expert. We were just experimenting ... in case Garracker decides to use those bulldozers on the City.'

'He won't,' said Benbow. 'He's changed his mind. He wants to find you.'

Dowie's eyes narrowed. 'Why? I don't understand. If Garracker means me no harm, why does he want to find me?'

'Because you're his clone,' said Benbow.

Dowie stared in disbelief. Trugg laid back her ears and growled.

'He had you cloned eleven years ago,' said Benbow. 'Then he had *me* cloned, to find *you*. These dogs are the result.' Briefly, he related Garracker's tale, wondering what would happen if Dowie didn't believe him. Or if, like Araby, he simply hated the whole idea of being a clone?

But Dowie's incredulous gaze slowly thawed into an exultant grin. Trugg's tail began to wag.

'Garracker's son! I *knew* I was someone special!'

'Clone,' growled Araby. 'Not son.'

'Clone, son ... it's all the same. I'm his heir, aren't I? And Garracker owns everything. *The lot*. How do I get to meet him? How soon?'

‘As soon as possible,’ said Benbow. ‘But you’re only one of three. Have you any idea where the other clones might be? Ever seen, or heard of, anyone who looks like you?’

Dowie shook his head slowly. ‘No. I would have remembered.’

‘I know the Recycler kept you for a while. Where were you before that? Who found you as a baby?’

‘No one. I found Nile’s gang, so I’m told: just crawled in one day. They adopted me. That was before Nile took over.’

‘Would anyone else remember?’

‘Come on, Benbow, it was ten years ago! There’s no one in the City over sixteen, except the Recycler, and she takes no notice of anything outside her yard. No one would remember it now.’

Benbow pondered. Dowie was probably telling the truth. However, he might not be in a hurry to find two other clones to share his good fortune . . . If you could call Garracker good fortune.

‘Have you any leads about the others? Any clues?’ asked Dowie, and looked satisfied when Benbow shook his head.

‘Nothing yet.’ One down, thought Benbow, but that was the easy one. Two were still to go.

Chapter Thirteen

Dowie went to Prospect Towers, and Garracker was pleased.

Three days later, a tank churned through the City streets, heaving over rusted cars until it juddered to a thunderous halt outside the Station. Garracker climbed out, cigar perched in a smiling mouth. On seeing Benbow, he threw his arms out wide.

'Benbow, my friend! I knew you wouldn't let me down. He's *perfect*. A real chip off the old block! Sharp as a knife, a born leader! He's had no education, of course, and his teeth are bad, but I'll see to all that. Can I come in?'

Benbow looked at Elise, who shrugged. Reluctantly, he nodded.

The Station was furnished for dogs, not people. Garracker sat on the only chair like a king on his throne and smiled on Benbow; then scowled at Wilf.

'Send that brat out, can't you?' he muttered. 'His face gives me the creeps.'

McCool ambled over to Wilf. 'How about a game of ball outside, kids?'

'We've got no ball,' objected Natty.

'We'll play potato, then.' McCool shepherded them out.

'To business,' said Garracker. 'You've found one

clone, Benbow, and I'm pleased. But what about the others?'

Benbow glanced at Elise. '*Your* case,' she murmured. He sighed, knowing his answer wouldn't satisfy Garracker.

'We've been searching the City,' he began, 'and asking around. We've questioned members of most of the gangs, but no one remembers any babies – or if they do, they're not saying. The trouble is, it's all too long ago. Most people old enough to remember that far back have left the City.'

'Then find them Outside.'

'Impossible.'

Garracker frowned. 'You're not giving up! If you can't cope, perhaps I should send men in to take over?'

'They wouldn't last long in the City,' said Benbow.

'Hah!' Garracker's eyes glittered. 'What about soldiers? Tanks? I think they'd cope, Benbow my friend. I could hire an army that would take this City apart! I'm strongly tempted, but for one thing – if my other clones are anything like Dowie, they'd fight back. I won't risk them getting killed.'

'But you'd risk the lives of all the other children, wouldn't you?' barked Araby. 'You don't care about *them*, only your clones!'

'How dare you speak to me like that?' snapped Garracker. 'Are all your pups as insolent as this one, Benbow?'

'Araby is young,' said Benbow.

'He's a young fool!'

Araby leapt to his feet. Benbow said quickly, 'He's not yet learned diplomacy. Araby – please go outside.'

Araby left, his lip curling. Daffodil sat mute and rigid; Elise, however, stretched out with the tired calm of age, quite unbothered.

'Benbow's doing his best to find your clones,' she told Garracker patiently. 'Give us a month. If he still hasn't succeeded, you can assume they're dead.'

'They are *not* dead!' Garracker's fists clenched.

'Wishing will not give them life,' said Elise.

'They are *not dead*! I know it. I *feel* it. They are in the City somewhere, and you will find them! And if you fail, Benbow, *your* clones will pay the price!'

This time it was Benbow who sprang to his feet, ears flattened, snarling. Garracker leapt from his chair and backed towards the door.

'*No*,' said Elise – but Benbow was too angry to think. He let instinct take over, running like fire through his body. How dare this arrogant man threaten three innocent pups? He wanted to seize Garracker and shake him like a rabbit.

The door crashed open. Araby barged through, barking frantically. 'Benbow! Benbow! Emergency!'

With a mighty effort, Benbow forced himself to dampen down his rage. 'What emergency? Where?' he rasped.

Araby's hair was standing on end. 'Fire! Fire in Burger Hall! There's smoke pouring out of the windows!'

'My tank!' cried Garracker. 'Out of my way!' Shoving past Araby, he stopped in the doorway to glare at Benbow.

'*Find my clones*. That's all you have to do. Just remember who is the dog here, and who the master!'

'Don't tell me my job,' growled Benbow, but Garracker had gone. Outside, the tank roared into noisy life.

'I hope it blows up!' snarled Araby.

'With him inside,' agreed Benbow.

'Enough!' said Elise. 'Benbow, there's a gang of children living over Burger Hall. You're the only ones who can help – all the other dogs are out on patrol.'

'I'm on it,' said Benbow. He galloped outside in time to see Garracker's tank thunder off with a trail of dust, heading away from the black cloud of smoke that frothed from Burger Hall.

'Benbow! Where are the fire engines?' cried Daffodil.

'Fire engines?' said Benbow grimly. 'What fire engines?'

'But . . .'

'No fire engines in the City,' said Benbow. 'No firemen: no policemen: no ambulances. Nothing but us. Haven't you worked that out yet? Everything that goes wrong, *we* have to fix.'

'But then how do we put it out?' wailed Daffodil.

'We don't,' said Benbow. 'We can't. We get everyone out, and let it burn.'

And with luck, he thought, the whole blazing pile won't collapse on top of us . . . Again, he had to push the memory away. He couldn't afford fear now.

'Look!' yelped Daffodil. 'Up on the roof!' On top of the building stood six small figures: five humans, waving wildly, and a dog. Benbow heard their faint shouts, as Natty came running over.

'The stairs are on fire!' she panted. 'There's a heap of rubbish burning on a landing. Sumitra's gang are up there, and they can't get down! They're stranded! We've got to save them, Benbow!'

Chapter Fourteen

'Sumitra?' bellowed Benbow. 'Where's your rope-walk?'

A thin wail floated downwards. 'Broken! We're stuck here! *Help!*'

'Natty, Daffodil: run back to the Station,' commanded Benbow. 'Fetch the rope-walk from the chest in the back room. And bring the cat.'

'Tonto?' asked Daffodil in surprise.

'No! The catapult.'

'I know,' said Natty, sprinting away.

'Now,' said Benbow, 'we need to get into the building next door.'

'McCool's already gone in,' Araby told him.

'Then go after him! Find a route to the top. Quickly!'

Araby ran off. Benbow sniffed at the smoke drifting in lazy billows from Burger Hall, and felt a deep unease. He smelt burning carpet – nothing strange about that, for old carpet still lay mouldering in some buildings – but why could he also smell burnt *paper*? And there was another, underlying stench that made his hackles rise: the sour, rough stink of alley-cats.

Araby reappeared. 'McCool's found an unblocked staircase next door.'

'And here's the rope-walk,' said Benbow, seeing Daffodil dragging it over by his teeth, loud and lumpy in a sack. Together the dogs hauled it into the next-door building and lugged it upstairs. It was ten flights to the top, and by the time they got there Benbow was wishing he'd retired.

'Let's get this across quickly,' he panted, as they emerged onto the flat roof. 'Pull the sack off, Daffodil. Take one end, Araby – Araby? What's wrong?'

Araby stood by the hatch, shivering, his tail between his legs. McCool glanced at him, shook his head and dragged the rope-walk to the roof's edge.

'Star of Araby?' queried Daffodil anxiously. 'What's the matter?' Araby didn't answer.

'Vertigo,' grunted McCool. 'Fear of heights. Leave him, he can't help us. *Hey, you over there!*' he shouted in Human across the chasm between the buildings. From the roof of Burger Hall, the children yelled back. They sounded scared, thought Benbow, but not panicky. Not yet.

Natty attached one end of the rope-walk to the stump of an old flagpole. Benbow unwound the rest, a long, clattering rope ladder with metal piping for rungs. Daffodil was quivering with excitement.

'Do you jump across, Admiral, with the end in your mouth?'

'You've got to be kidding,' said Benbow. 'We use the cat.'

Swiftly he threaded the loose end of the rope-walk into the catapult, and set the spring. Aiming it carefully, he released the catch. With a mighty PYOING the rope-walk sprang like a cluster of flying snakes across the gap. The children on the far side scrambled to retrieve it, and hooked it over a ventilation shaft.

A moment later, the smallest girl was clambering on all fours across the swaying, rattling bridge. Three more children followed, clinging like monkeys to the rungs as the rope-walk jangled. Then just one girl was left, along with the dog – a small, shivering mongrel.

'Come on, Sumitra!' Natty shouted.

'That dog can't cross,' said McCool under his breath.

'She'll have to carry him,' said Benbow, and indeed Sumitra was trying to pick up the dog, which wriggled and howled in protest. Behind her, a sudden flame licked up from the ventilation shaft, darting skywards like a lizard's tongue.

Benbow cursed himself. 'I should have told Natty to bring the dog sling,' he groaned. 'I forgot all about it. They can't cross like that!'

Clutching the dog in both arms, Sumitra set an experimental foot on the first rung. The rope-walk shuddered and rang like a peal of bells. Benbow began to bark a warning; but a shout forestalled him.

'Stop, Sumitra! Stop!'

Benbow was amazed. It was Wilf who had shouted – Wilf, who never spoke above a murmur. Wilf was scampering along the rope-walk – almost *running* – with a sure-footedness that made Benbow blink.

At the far side, Wilf pulled off his ragged sweater, and knotted the sleeves together. Ignoring the bursts of flame that belched from the ventilation shaft, he looped the sleeves around his neck, then tucked the sweater's collar in his belt.

'There!' he said, taking the unwilling dog from Sumitra and stashing it into the improvised sling. He followed Sumitra back across the swaying rope-walk, more slowly this time, with the dog howling all the way.

'Well done, Wilf,' said Natty proudly, as she lifted the dog out. It snapped at her fingers, yapped angrily at Wilf and raced after its human companions, who were already climbing down the hatchway.

'Well! They didn't even say thank you!' huffed Daffodil. 'I was brought up to always say please and thank you for *everything*!'

'That explains a lot,' Benbow muttered.

'Hey, you there!' scolded Daffodil. 'Can't you even stop to thank us?'

'No time!' cried Sumitra. 'Get out now, before he fires this building too!'

'Who?'

'The fire-starter!'

'Fire-starter?' asked Daffodil blankly. But Benbow barked in consternation,

'Downstairs, everyone! We'll retrieve the rope-walk later. Quickly, Natty! Hurry up, McCool! Araby! Wake up!'

Araby still crouched, immobile, by the hatch. An occasional shiver ran across his flanks. He stared at Benbow with miserable eyes.

'Araby!' barked Benbow. 'Snap out of it!'

'C'mon, bro,' said McCool more gently. 'We're going down. Down, OK? You'll be all right in a minute.' He nudged Araby into trembling movement, and the dogs descended together.

But halfway down the stairs, they found Sumitra's gang in a frightened huddle on the landing. A pile of rubbish was burning fiercely, blocking their path. The children shrank back from the flames' mad, crackling dance.

Then, on the far side of the fire, Benbow saw something that made his hair stand on end: a boy, bobbing and swaying, copying the dance of the flames – a boy who brandished a blazing stick in wild triumph.

'The fire-starter!' Sumitra whispered.

Benbow was filled with a rage so great that he forgot his human voice. With a furious *woof!* he leapt right across the fire. His jaws snapped with a crunch that would have broken bone – but met instead the boy's flaming brand. Benbow glimpsed a soot-smeared face, heard a squeal, smelt the disquieting reek of *cat* – and then his own fur burning.

He let go and dropped to the ground, rolling over to extinguish the flames on his coat. Spent matches lay scattered on the floor around him. Before he could rise, the boy screamed, and jumped down the stairs three at a time.

Benbow shook himself, took a leap after the boy, then halted. The children were still trapped on the wrong side of the flames.

He turned back and barked. 'Carpet! There's some on the next floor. Fetch it!' McCool was already dashing away, and returned a moment later dragging a sodden length of carpet. The children up-ended it and let it topple onto the fire.

The flames sizzled away into acrid smoke and hissing steam. Scrambling over the fizzing carpet, the children dived through the smoke and down the stairs. Benbow followed as fast as his plastic leg would allow.

Too late. When he got outside, there was no sign of the fire-starter.

'Circle the building!' he barked. The dogs trawled the streets around Burger Hall, noses to the ground, but without result.

'He had too much of a head start,' panted McCool regretfully. 'I can't find a trail. He must know all the short cuts and hidey-holes. Wish I did.'

'He's gone,' growled Araby sullenly. 'There's nothing we can do.'

'Nothing we can do?' said Benbow sharply. 'What sort of attitude is that? We're police dogs! We can hunt him down!'

'But aren't we meant to be looking for the clones?' asked Daffodil anxiously. 'Garracker said—'

'I don't give a rat's snout what Garracker said! There's a fire-starter on the loose, and we're going to catch him!'

'Garracker won't like it,' muttered Araby.

Benbow rounded on him, snarling so ferociously that Araby ducked. 'We're police dogs, not lap-dogs! If Garracker doesn't like it, too bad! You think I'm going to watch the towers and all the children burn?'

'Oh, no,' said Daffodil.

'We can't do that,' agreed McCool. 'Can we, bro?' He nosed at Araby, who nodded slow agreement.

'Then it's decided,' barked Benbow. 'We're going to find the fire-starter!'

Chapter Fifteen

'What are you looking for, Admiral?'

'Cats and smoke,' muttered Benbow. 'He's here, I know it. But who is he?'

He gazed up at the Museum. Cats dozed in pools of weak sunshine, sprawled in unlikely poses along the lower window-ledges. Behind the drowsing cats, the windows were solidly bricked up.

'Dog Two says they call him Slane,' said McCool offhandedly.

'*Who?*'

'Dog Two. You know, the Recycler's— '

'No, *Slane*!'

'Oh . . . stinks of cat, lurks in corners, creeps around by himself, Dog Two says. A loner and a thief.'

'Isn't he in a gang?'

McCool shrugged. 'Maybe none'll have him.'

'But if he's here,' growled Benbow, 'how does he get in?' He frowned at the doorway, which was bricked up as securely as the windows. There were no cracks in the walls: this place was built to last. Impregnable. Yet, behind the Museum smells of smoke and cat and stone, lay another scent, faint as a moonshadow, that made the fur rise on his neck.

'This is a wild goose chase,' muttered Araby. 'What about Garracker's clones?' Daffodil glanced anxiously at

Benbow, who pretended not to hear, but studied the stone lions carved over the door, considering.

'That's the Town Hall crest,' said Benbow suddenly. 'We need to talk to Dowie.'

The baffled pups trailed after him to the Town Hall. Inside, the market was back in place, its stalls set up on marble tiles swept as clean as if the collapse of the potato crop had never happened. The sickly-sweet smell that Benbow had noticed last time still hung around the place.

As he headed for the stairs, the two huge mastiffs quickly barred his way. Between them, the bull terrier, Trugg, fixed the police dogs with a belligerent eye.

'We've come to see Dowie,' said Benbow. 'Is he here?'

Trugg thought about it. 'Yup,' she said, and twitched an ear at a mastiff, who loped away.

'Can we go up?'

'Nope.'

'Shall we wait?'

'Yup.' Trugg sat down, watching them intently.

'Do you like it here?' asked Daffodil politely.

'Yup.'

'Can't you say anything but Nope and Yup?' demanded Araby in irritation.

'Yup.'

'Go on, then.'

'Nope.'

'Brains of a peanut,' grumbled Araby. Benbow rounded on him.

'Shame on you, Araby! How unfair! You speak

excellent Human – but have you forgotten how to understand Dog? Don't you know there are a hundred meanings to every Nope and Yup? And not every dog *likes* dogs who talk Human—'

'Nope.'

' – think we're uppity know-all poodles.'

'Yup.'

Araby's ears flattened against his skull. But before he could answer, Dowie came downstairs: a happy, satisfied and generous Dowie.

'Benbow! My friend! What can I do for you?'

'I'm glad to find you here,' said Benbow. 'I thought you might be with Garracker.'

'Ah, yes.' A faraway look came into Dowie's eyes. 'My other, older self. I'm enjoying myself with Garracker. He has some interesting plans. Well, so do I! I'm not moving out of here just yet.'

'Do you get on well with him?' asked Daffodil wistfully. 'It's very important to get on with your family.' He cast a reproachful glance at Araby.

'Like a house on fire,' said Dowie, grinning.

'Speaking of fires,' said Benbow, 'we've got a fire-starter.'

Dowie's face turned dark. 'I knew it,' he muttered. 'Those fires in my warehouses – they weren't accidental. Who is it? Do you know?'

'We think he's called Slane, and lives in the Museum.'

'Slane?' Dowie frowned. 'Filthy, stinks, bites people?'

'Probably.'

'The Museum's impenetrable. No way in,' said Dowie.

'Believe me, I've tried – I could use a strong building like that.'

'The Town Hall and the Museum were built by the same humans, long ago,' said Benbow. 'Could there be any way into the Museum from here?'

Dowie rubbed his chin. 'Well – there are the old air-raid shelters, but they're all blocked up.'

'Air-raid shelters?' whispered Daffodil. 'What are those?'

Dowie overheard him. 'They're places people used to hide in wartime,' he said. 'Long ago – I don't know when. They're tunnels running off our basement. Like I said, though, they're all blocked. Anyway, if Slane was coming in and out that way, I think we would have noticed.'

'Can we look in your basement?' asked Benbow.

'If you like. But don't frighten the pigs.'

Trugg led them down a flight of dank stone steps. As they descended, the sickly-sweet smell became over-powering.

'That's pig, is it?' muttered Benbow.

'Yup.'

'Well, that's one smell I'll never forget.'

'Nope.'

As his eyes adjusted to the darkness, Benbow saw that the basement was divided into a dozen doorless rooms. Pigs wandered from one to another, grunting and snuffling in the gloom, and soon an interested herd had gathered to watch the dogs with intelligent eyes.

'Wonder if I could learn Pig?' mused McCool, and gave an experimental grunt.

'We're looking for a tunnel,' said Benbow firmly.

'It's here,' said Dowie, holding up a torch to a dark opening in the wall.

The tunnel was wide and low, and lined with slimy brick. The dogs entered nervously, but could go only a few steps before they met a heap of stone blocks and wooden beams rammed against their path, leaving only the smallest gap. Benbow put his nose to the blackness, and sniffed, trying to reach beyond the overwhelming tide of pig.

'Wet brick,' he murmured, 'black beetles, rats, there's a toad somewhere . . . The air seems fresh. Too fresh for a dead end.' He paused, closing his eyes, and inhaled again.

'Smoke in the distance,' he said at last. 'And *cats*. I'm sure of it.' He opened his eyes. 'We need to get in there, somehow.'

'Are we going to look for this fire-starter *now*?' complained Araby. 'I thought— '

'You thought what?'

'Well . . . that we . . . that Garracker . . . ' As Benbow gazed at him without reply, Araby's voice trailed away.

'The Admiral knows best,' said Daffodil firmly.

'Could Trugg squeeze through that gap?' asked McCool.

'*Nope!*' said Trugg indignantly.

'Too narrow,' agreed Benbow.

'What about a smaller dog?' suggested Daffodil. 'A Yorkshire terrier?'

'Maybe. But we couldn't send a Yorkie in with all those cats. It wouldn't last a minute!'

'What we need,' remarked McCool, 'is another cat.'

'No cats here,' said Dowie. 'The dogs won't stand for it.'

'We're stuck, then,' grunted Araby.

But Benbow chuckled suddenly. 'Oh, no, we're not. You're forgetting someone. Tonto!'

Chapter Sixteen

'*No!*' hissed Tonto. His fur stood up like bristles on a broom. 'Absolutely not!'

'It's not dangerous. We only want you to have a little look, to see if there's another entrance,' Benbow pleaded. 'You won't meet anyone, except a few cats.'

'Alley-cats,' sniffed Tonto.

'It's worth a tin of cat-food,' offered McCool.

'Hang on!' protested Benbow. 'Where are we going to get cat-food? The Recycler doesn't do cat-food.'

McCool shrugged. 'Ask Garracker?'

'Just think of it, Tonto,' said Daffodil. 'A whole day without rat!'

Tonto's eyes narrowed. 'I want a week.'

'A *week*?'

'In advance. Slinkypuss with salmon. I'll only do it for Slinkypuss. Eight tins.'

'*Eight?*'

'Ten,' said Tonto sleekly. 'May as well round it up.'

'Done!' said McCool hurriedly, before the price went up again.

'Really?' grumbled Benbow. 'Well, *you* can send a message to Garracker, telling him that ten tins of Slinkypuss are vital to our investigations. What are you waiting for?' He glared at McCool until the younger dog backed away. 'And your coat still needs a trim!' Benbow barked after him.

Tonto began to clean his whiskers. 'No offence, dear Benbow, but have you noticed how your clones keep overriding you? Inevitable, I suppose, when an elderly cripple tries to keep pace with three young pups.' He sat down and licked himself delicately.

Araby murmured to Benbow. 'Can Tonto be trusted?'

'As much as any cat can.'

'I don't want to be unfair,' said Araby hesitantly, 'but is it safe to pay him in advance?'

'Where Tonto's concerned, you can be as unfair as you like. No, it's not safe. He's going to work for his Slinkypuss.'

So, next evening, after ten tins of cat-food had been delivered to the Town Hall by tank, Tonto was escorted there by the dogs. Down in the warm, rank basement, they hustled him past the sleepy pigs to the dark tunnel.

At the tunnel's mouth lay a clump of tins, with Trugg resting her front paws on them.

'I said, *in advance*,' objected Tonto.

'You've got them in advance. They're here. You can eat them as soon as you've done the job.'

'It's dark,' sulked Tonto.

'Best time. Cats like the dark,' said Benbow.

Tonto glowered at the dogs. 'No offence,' he hissed, 'but you're a load of insensitive bullies.' Trotting down the tunnel, he leapt lightly up to the hole in the tumbled stone, and slipped through it like a hand into a glove. He was gone without a sound.

'I'll wait outside in case he finds another exit in the street,' said Daffodil eagerly.

'He's more likely to come back *here*,' said Benbow, 'pretending he's looked when he's just been skulking on the other side of that hole. But I shall know by his smell.' He spoke loudly, directing his voice at the wall. 'I shall expect Tonto to come back smelling of smoke and alley-cat. I shall stay here and wait.'

'Me too,' said Araby. He looked at Trugg, and lowered his head submissively. 'Would you like to keep us company?'

'Nope.' She stuck her tail high in the air and marched off.

McCool wandered away to grunt at some pigs, leaving Araby and Benbow together at the tunnel's mouth. Araby lay down dejectedly, nose on paws.

'*That* didn't work,' he said.

'Don't expect to get everything right all at once,' said Benbow gently. He felt uncomfortably aware that he'd been hard on Araby – too hard, perhaps.

'Don't seem to be getting anything right,' Araby mumbled into his paws. 'My foster-parents told me what a great police dog I'd be – as if I was born knowing everything about it. I thought it would be easy. But I'm not much good at all.'

Benbow sat beside him. 'You can't tell yet,' he said. 'Nobody's born a good police dog, even the clone of one. It's experience that counts. You just need to learn how to handle situations.'

'Not doing too well so far,' said Araby in a muffled voice.

Benbow recognised his own tendency to mope when

things went wrong. He said bracingly, 'I expect Trugg will come round. She's got to maintain her dignity, that's all.'

'I wasn't thinking of Trugg,' said Araby. 'I was thinking of – of – up on the roof yesterday.' His voice dropped. 'I just couldn't move. Whenever I looked at the edge, my head began to spin, and I kept thinking I was going to fall off. I felt sick. It was terrible. I don't understand why it happened. The others were all right. *You're* not afraid of heights, are you?'

'I'm not keen on them, but they don't make me...' Benbow paused, trying to think of a more tactful word than *panic*. '...anxious,' he said at last. 'Perhaps you got frightened by a high place when you were very young?'

Araby shook his head. 'I don't remember. I feel so ashamed. I can't stand weakness! I hate being weak. Don't you feel the same, with your—' He looked askance at Benbow's plastic leg.

Benbow looked at it too. 'I don't hate it. I'm stuck with it, so there's no point hating it. It's just a nuisance.'

Araby shivered. 'I couldn't stand it.'

'Like you can't stand being a clone?'

Araby turned his head away. 'I know I've been rude,' he muttered. 'It's just...I've always thought I was special; unique. My foster-parents always told me so. And now I find out I'm identical to three other dogs.'

'But you're not!' said Benbow. 'Your being scared of heights just proves you're different!'

'I don't want to be different like *that*!'

Benbow wondered how to comfort him. 'I expect you'll find a way to cope.'

'How?' groaned Araby.

A little desperately, Benbow racked his brains. 'Practise. Look out of first-storey windows until it doesn't bother you, then work your way up – second floor, and so on. I'm sure you'll overcome your fear.'

'You think so?' asked Araby hopefully.

'Definitely.'

Araby sat up a little straighter. 'I'll try it.'

'You know, I couldn't stand the thought of being cloned either,' Benbow admitted. 'I hated the idea. I expected three interchangeable little Benbows, all alike in thought and deed – but you're all different, and I don't know why... Some of it's down to your foster homes, I suppose. But you're just different, anyway.' He thought about the aspects of himself that he recognised in the clones: Araby had his pride and impatience, and McCool the careless curiosity of his youth... but Daffodil?

'Daffodil's very like you,' said Araby, as if reading his thoughts.

'*Is* he? *How*?'

'Trying to do the right thing all the time.'

'I wish he'd stop calling me Admiral.'

Araby laughed. 'Then why don't you ask him to stop? I'll tell you why – because you're too polite. Just like him.' He stood up and shook himself, looking more cheerful. 'With all these pigs around, do you think they might have a bacon chop anywhere?'

'Go and ask.' Benbow watched Araby wander away. Not a bad-looking dog after all, he thought, if you ignored the strange mouth, and the lopsided ear...Lean and strong, well put together.

Benbow rolled over, feeling far from lean and strong himself. He yawned hugely, then opened his eyes wide and fixed them on the tunnel. His sense of smell had already shut down, suffering from pig overload, and his eyelids were drooping again when Daffodil barked him into wakefulness.

'Admiral! Admiral! He's back!'

He stretched. 'Call me Benbow, Daff.'

'What? Oh! Right. Tonto's back! He just walked in upstairs. He's found another entrance!'

Calling to the dogs, Benbow ran up to the marbled hall. Tonto swaggered over, whiskers twitching disdainfully.

'Nothing to it!' he sniffed. 'If you dumb dogs had looked a bit harder you would have found the entrance yourself.'

'Where is it?'

'I want my Slinkypuss.'

'Your job's only half done,' growled Benbow. 'Show us the entrance, and you'll get your tins.'

Tonto examined an elegant paw. 'Actually, I've decided the Slinkypuss isn't enough. I want to sleep in your basket tonight, Benbow.'

'You just try it,' retorted Benbow.

'And tomorrow night,' said Tonto, beginning to arch and huff.

'Oh, all right! All right!'

'By the stove.'

'*Yes!* Just tell us where the entrance is!'

'I'll take you there,' said Tonto. 'Well, come along! Dear me, you dogs are so slow.'

Dowie came hurrying over with Camilla. 'You've found a way in?' he asked.

'I hope so,' said Benbow. 'We'll try it now. Slane might be asleep.'

'I'd like to come with you,' said Dowie regretfully. 'But I'm going to Prospect Towers, to dine with my ancestor.'

'Garracker?'

'That's right. Good food, and a bit of fun.' Seeing Benbow's puzzled expression, Dowie laughed. 'It's so easy!' he said. 'I can make him do whatever I want. I know all the buttons to press. But take Trugg with you, and Camilla.'

'Just in case you need anything blowing up,' said Camilla. She waved a large canvas bag with a grin. 'It's all here. Fuses, detonators—'

'Oh, be careful, please!' begged Daffodil.

'Don't worry! I know what I'm doing.'

Outside, darkness had fallen. A single, spluttering oil-lamp lit up the fountain; beyond it, the night was a black wall dotted with an occasional flickering light, like a shifty eye. The moon hid behind swirling clouds.

'We need torches,' said Benbow. 'I should have thought.' As he spoke, feet came running through the dark, and Natty and Wilf emerged into the lamplight, carrying handfuls of torches, police dog issue, on wide headbands.

'We brought you these,' panted Natty. She began to fasten them around the dogs' heads.

'And we're coming with you,' added Wilf.

Tonto sat down to groom himself. 'No offence, Benbow, but your patrols are turning into a regular circus. What a fuss – all for some silly boy with a box of matches.'

'The Admiral – I mean Benbow – is doing *real* police work,' said Daffodil severely.

'He can do what he likes,' added McCool. 'He's a free spirit.'

'Is he?' said Tonto. 'I thought he was Garracker's little obedient doggie. No offence, Benbow. But if Garracker gets to hear about this, won't that mean your jobs are on the line? Or even your heads?' He stared at Benbow, his eyes yellow in the lamplight. 'More to the point – when Garracker's got rid of you lot, and the Station's empty – where will *I* live, Benbow?'

Chapter Seventeen

Tonto led them down Empire Row, turned left opposite the Museum, and stopped by an ivy-covered ruin.

'But this is the Library,' said Benbow. 'This can't be the place.'

'Nope.'

'Yes!' hissed Tonto. 'Downstairs!'

Benbow shone his torch inside, then carefully began to thread his way through the tangle of brambles and hidden wires. 'Mind the snares!' he called.

'Nice design,' said Wilf, looking at them thoughtfully.

Benbow peered down the stairwell. The stairs had collapsed in a jagged heap of concrete. 'Downstairs, Tonto? Not even a rat could squeeze through there!'

'That's where you're wrong, dunderhead,' retorted Tonto. 'No offence. I'm just a little stressed after my difficult and dangerous journey. That tunnel was full of rats. Then I reached a fork where the air was moving, and I heard cats going to and fro. From their talk, I knew the right fork led to the Museum: so I took the left one, and came out here.'

'What, up that stairwell?' said McCool.

'Certainly,' sniffed Tonto. 'We cats can slide through holes you couldn't even get your fat nose into.'

'Maybe,' said Benbow. 'But don't tell me Slane uses that route.'

'I could blast a way through,' suggested Camilla.

'No! Too noisy, and too dangerous.'

'You're all blind.' Tonto stalked through the thicket of snares until he reached a doorway in the corner. 'There you are,' he said. '*That's* Slane's way.'

Tiptoeing after him, Natty stuck her torch inside. 'But there's no floor!'

'Dear me,' said Tonto, rolling his eyes. 'It's a lift shaft.'

'I can't see a lift. Is there a ladder?' Natty shone her torch around the walls. A couple of lengths of thin rope dangled down one side. 'He couldn't climb that,' she said doubtfully. 'It wouldn't hold his weight.'

'*I* know!' said Wilf suddenly, leaning out into the lift shaft. Benbow, startled, clamped his teeth onto a mouthful of Wilf's jumper – which stank of ointment and dog-blanket – as Wilf grabbed the nearest cord and tugged.

It came reeling down, while the further cord shot up, revealing a thick rope tied to its end. As Wilf pulled, the rope travelled up the lift shaft and over an unseen pulley at the top, to come back down into his hand.

'So he climbs up this?' said Daffodil.

'Yup,' said Trugg.

'No,' said Wilf. He hauled on the rope, arm over arm, until, slow as a snail, a platform came inching up the lift shaft. 'He's made his own lift,' he said happily. 'It's brilliant! Jump on!'

'Jump on?' repeated Benbow. The platform was an old door, tied on all sides with huge, balled knots. He didn't fancy jumping onto *that*.

Wilf stepped carefully onto the platform, still gripping his rope tight.

'Not all at once,' he said. 'Three of you.'

Araby stepped on. 'I'll go first. I'm only scared of going up, not down.'

'Me too,' said Camilla.

'Yup,' said Trugg. Gingerly they sat on the platform, and Wilf began to let out his rope, hand over hand. As gradually as the setting sun, the platform sank out of sight.

Benbow watched it disappear into darkness. At last a call came echoing up the shaft. 'We're at the bottom!'

The ropes started moving again. The sluggish platform, with Wilf hauling away, crept back to Benbow's level. McCool, Tonto and Natty climbed on and were transported down.

Benbow and Daffodil were last. Daffodil, visibly nervous, needed several attempts to step onto the platform.

'I don't understand,' he whispered, 'how Wilf can hold our weight.'

'Technology,' whispered back Benbow, who didn't understand either. 'It's a human thing.'

'Pulleys,' said Wilf confidently. 'For every armful of rope I let out, we only go down a fraction. But we only weigh a fraction as much, because of all the pulleys. I'd like to make something like this.' His eye shone.

'Well, well,' said Benbow. 'The things you humans think of.' He couldn't wait to reach the bottom, and hardly breathed until the platform landed with a thud. The others stood waiting, shadowy behind their lamps.

'Seen what's down here, Benbow?' said Araby quietly.

Benbow swung his head round, and was astounded.

'Tonto – you never mentioned this!'

'Mentioned what?'

'*Books!*'

'Oh, those,' said Tonto with contempt. 'Mouse food.'

Bookshelves stretched away as far as the light would reach. Benbow tried to remember when he'd last seen a book in the City... occasionally at the Recycler's, maybe, being sold as toilet paper, or fire-lighters...

There were a lot of fire-lighters here. Many shelves were half empty; books lay on the floor, ripped in two. Mice hadn't done *that*.

'Come on,' said Tonto impatiently, diving into a passage beyond the bookshelves. At once the damp brick walls changed to rough-hewn sandstone. They passed the rusty bones of an iron bedstead that still held a mildewed mattress.

'Weird,' said McCool.

Then the tunnel branched, as Tonto had promised. On the wall a stained notice read:

MUSEUM AIR-RAID SHELTERS
A GENUINE WORLD WAR II EXPERIENCE
TOURS TWICE DAILY

On either side, tunnels ran off into blackness. The air was colder than stone. Yet, away in the dark, Benbow thought he heard a faint flicker of human voices, and a snatch of song, that, as soon as he caught it, faded like the music on Elise's radio when the batteries were flat.

'Can you hear something?' he asked.

'No,' said McCool. 'Should I?' But Araby said quietly,

'This place is full of ghosts. My hair's standing on end.'

Benbow realised that his was too. They hurried on without speaking until the sandstone turned to brick again, and the fur on Benbow's neck lay down.

Soon the brick changed to white tiles that reminded him so strongly of the hospital that his leg began to ache. The corridor was lined with doors; when they peered in, they saw small rooms crammed with stuffed birds and animals, glass cases full of butterflies, and the grinning skeleton of a sheep.

Natty was enraptured. 'Treasure!' she breathed. 'Can I stay and look?'

'Not now,' said Benbow. 'We need speed, and strength, and secrecy, if we're to catch Slane unawares.' They hurried on down the corridor to a narrow staircase.

'Dip your lights,' said Benbow quietly, but too late. They had been seen. Two cats whisked out of the darkness under the stairs and fled upwards with angry wails.

'So much for secrecy,' said Benbow. 'But we've still got strength. Charge!'

He galloped upstairs as fast as his leg would allow, but his clones soon outstripped him. At the top, he stopped and caught his breath, amazed.

The torchlight pooled into a great chamber, glimmering on dozens of glass cases. Benbow had never seen so much unbroken glass inside the City. Ahead of them stretched a silent avenue of statues, graceful and pensive. They had entered the Museum.

'Natty, Wilf – stay here,' commanded Benbow. 'If you see Slane, shout! Don't let him get down the stairs! Everyone else, spread out. Bark if you see anything.'

The dogs loped off in all directions. Benbow took a path between the ranks of statues, with Trugg to his right. The hair on his back was rising again; all his senses were quivering. The statues cast black shadows that swayed in the torchlight, and the smell of cat was very strong.

Then – without warning – something thudded onto Benbow's back, tearing at his fur. Half a dozen furred, clawed bombs landed on him, yowling. *Cats.*

Benbow snapped and snarled, shaking himself frantically to try and loosen their grip. As two fell off, he batted them away with his paws, but more cats took their place, scratching and biting him unmercifully. Their claws gouged his back like thorns; one clung to his head and bit his ear.

From the corner of his eye, Benbow saw Trugg pounding towards him. As she leapt on his back, he staggered under the sudden weight. Then he heard Trugg's jaws crunch, and a dead cat was tossed away. After the second crunch, the other cats fled.

'Thanks, Trugg,' panted Benbow, as the bull terrier jumped down. 'After 'em?'

'Yup!' They charged off in pursuit, Benbow thinking that the cats might lead him to Slane.

But suddenly the cats slipped away, melting into the darkness. Benbow pulled up by the last statue, panting in angry bewilderment, not knowing which way to go.

Without warning, a blow crashed down upon his side. He staggered, and heard a triumphant screech.

'Slane!' he gasped. It was the fire-starter all right; fierce and wild and filthy, with that worrying scent... Slane danced awkwardly from leg to leg, waving a cudgel, uttering strange bird-like cries. Benbow leapt at his chest, aiming to pin him down. Slane swung his club, and hit Benbow with a speed and force that took him by surprise. The blow knocked him sideways, and his leg fell off.

Trugg let out a volley of loud, hoarse barks. Then, as Slane clubbed Benbow a third time, she buried her teeth in his leg. Slane shrieked, dropped his stick and tried to run, with Trugg clamped to his shin. Within seconds he was surrounded by Benbow's clones. He backed up against a statue, moaning and shivering.

'Steady!' said Benbow, struggling to his feet. He shone his torch full on the wincing, twitching face, trying to see beneath the dirt, while his sense of smell sent a warning rocketing to his brain. 'Don't bite him,' he said thickly. 'He's—'

His words were drowned out by a terrific crash. The dogs all ducked instinctively, and Slane set up a long wail.

The wall of the Museum burst open. Its stones flew through the air in a silver shower, gleaming like ice in the moonlight.

Benbow swore, furiously. 'Camilla and her blasted bombs! What does she think she's playing at! I told her—'

The words died in his throat. From beyond the broken wall came a harsh, throaty rumble. An *engine*. More stones tumbled down. Then through the gap surged a black and deafening monster with dazzling yellow eyes.

Garracker's tank.

Chapter Eighteen

Benbow thought the tank would never stop. But at last, with a long, grinding squeal, it halted just metres away. Its hatch opened and Garracker jumped down. Behind him, Dowie climbed out stealthily, and slipped away.

Garracker advanced on Benbow, a looming black shadow silhouetted against the tank's headlights.

'I told you to *find my clones*!'

Benbow stared at him unwaveringly, and said nothing.

'What's going on?' roared Garracker. 'What are you doing here?'

'Making the City safe to live in,' answered Benbow quietly.

'I'll tell you who's not safe!' spat Garracker. '*You!* You and your misbegotten pups! You had orders, Benbow. Now Dowie tells me you're chasing cats around the Museum! *What the devil do you think you're doing?*'

'Finding your clones,' said Benbow. He swung his torch round onto the blinking, shivering Slane. 'Garracker: meet Slane. Clone number two.'

Garracker froze, still as the statues around him. Slane's eyes slid past Garracker, squinted at the tank, then shifted from dog to dog, blank as rolling marbles. He scratched himself and began to moan quietly.

'*He's* not mine,' said Garracker, his voice cracking.

'Take him home,' answered Benbow. He felt as cold

and tired as winter. 'Clean him up. Have a good look. Clone number two, Garracker.' He picked up his leg and limped out of the tank's ruthless glare to strap it back on.

Daffodil whispered to him, 'Did you know all along?'

'I wasn't sure till now... I just knew there was something wrong about his smell. Beneath the dirt and smoke and cat, it's Garracker's.'

Garracker appeared to be glued to the ground. But Dowie strolled out of the shadows where he had been muttering to Camilla, and walked over to examine Slane.

'Hello, there,' he said conversationally. His face sharpened, as if inspecting itself in a smeared and dirty mirror.

'I'm your brother,' he said. 'I'm Dowie. You may have heard of me. Or you may not. *Can* you hear? Can you *talk*?'

Slane was silent, eyes sliding, limp hands twitching.

'He can't talk,' said Dowie lightly. 'What a pity.'

'Get out of the way!' said Garracker hoarsely. Pushing Dowie aside, he dropped on one knee beside Slane. 'Son? Can you hear me? Say something! Say your name to me. *Slane*. Say it. You're Slane,' he repeated.

Slane began to mumble and stutter. Benbow strained to hear words. There were none; only sounds.

'I'm afraid he won't be much use to you,' said Dowie gravely. As he turned away, he broke into a fierce grin.

'That'll teach him!' he muttered. 'Thinks he can boss me around! Thinks he owns me! Do this, do that, go there. Thinks he owns the City as well. Wants me to leave! No way! I don't like his office blocks. I like things the way they are.' The smile collapsed into a resentful frown, as Dowie cracked his knuckles angrily.

Slane was still jabbering, arms waving in loose gestures that Benbow couldn't understand. When Araby moved too close, Slane hissed and spat.

'Barely human,' said McCool soberly. 'I wonder what happened to him? Who brought him up?'

'No one, I'd guess,' said Benbow.

'No. Cats, maybe.'

Watching Slane, Benbow could believe it. What had the boy lived on, all these years? *Rat?* He shuddered.

'Go home,' he told Natty and Wilf tersely. He didn't think the sight of Slane was good for them; and he felt dimly afraid of what Garracker might do.

But Wilf, staring fascinated at Slane, said, 'No, not yet! I want to hear what he says.'

'Slane? He's saying nothing,' said Benbow.

'He's almost talking,' argued Wilf. 'Listen to him! He made that lift, remember? He *knows* things!'

Slane flapped his hands, jerking his head at the tank.

'You like my tank?' said Garracker, speaking with desperate, measured care. 'Come and look at it. Come and see my tank, Slane. Maybe you could have a ride.' He grasped Slane's hand, and Slane took two hesitant steps.

'Ooops!' said Dowie. He ran towards them, crying, 'No! That's not a good idea! Stay away from that tank, it's—'

There was a loud WHOOMP, and the tank appeared to leap sideways. When it settled again, the left side sat lower than the right. A lot lower.

'Wonderful girl, Camilla,' breathed Dowie.

'My tank! *You've blown up my tank!*'

'Just teaching you a lesson,' retorted Dowie. 'You've been rampaging through my City too freely with that tank, knocking over everything in sight.'

'It's not your City! It's mine!'

'Oh, yes? Then tell me where Brewer's Yard is? Where does Angel live? How many gangs are there in Grindle Heights?' Dowie fired at him. 'How do you get from Bean Street to Lark Lane without a broken leg?'

'Shut up! Shut up!' roared Garracker. Trugg stood in front of Dowie and growled a deep warning. Slane began to make a noise like a crow.

'Shut your dog up, too!' yelled Garracker. 'I'm ashamed to have bred you! You're no son of mine!'

'That's right,' said Dowie. 'I'm not your son. I'm *you*, Garracker. And so is Slane. That's *you* – without your office blocks and tanks and safes full of money. Take a good look at him. Like what you see?'

Garracker was speechless.

'You may have made me,' shouted Dowie, 'but you don't own me, or the City! If you owned us, you'd look after us. Do you? No! You want to tear down the City and throw away its people! *I* look after the City. *I* own the City. So does Angel, and Greenspan, and Benbow here.'

'Hang on,' said Benbow, startled, 'leave me out of it.'

'How could I look after you?' said Garracker hoarsely. 'I'd lost you! I thought you were dead! But I found you, didn't I? At great expense, too!'

Dowie's lip curled. 'Is that what bothers you? The

expense? Well, don't spend any more on *me*. You want a son and heir? Have Slane. He's all yours. Trugg? Cam? Let's get out of here.'

The three of them marched towards the gap in the wall. Camilla stuck her tongue out at Garracker as she passed.

'How dare you?' yelled Garracker. 'I *made* you! Dowie! Come back here – *I order you!*' Then, cursing, he ran after Dowie, blundering past the broken hulk of his tank, and jumped through the shattered wall into the moonlight.

'Garracker! Stop!' barked Benbow, but Garracker had gone. 'He's crazy! Does he think he can catch them? He'll be lost in two minutes!'

'Shall I go after him?' asked Araby.

'No. Stay here and guard Slane!' Hobbling painfully – for he was stiff and sore where Slane had hit him, and his missing leg throbbed like a bad memory – Benbow lumbered to the wall and peered out.

Although the moonlit tower-tops glistened palely, the streets below were wells of darkness where the moon could never reach. There was no movement in their black depths, only the hollow sound of clattering feet – Garracker's feet, thought Benbow, judging by their heaviness and the way they stumbled, unused to the dark.

The footsteps faltered, then ceased altogether. There was a faint slither, and a rattle; and a scream ripped through the air.

'I'm coming!' barked Benbow, as he leapt from the wall. Garracker's incoherent shouts began to echo round the silent towers. Running through the tiny puddle of light made by his torch, Benbow followed the noise to a side-alley shrouded in blackness.

'Get me down! Get me down!' yelled Garracker's voice. Benbow shone his torch upwards. Garracker swung slowly through its beam, upside down, hanging from a rope around his ankle. Away in the shadows rang a peal of cold laughter.

McCool and Wilf came running up behind him. Wilf gasped as he saw Garracker, swinging like a giant pendulum.

'Don't worry! I'll cut you down!' he cried, and darted down the alley, skipping nimbly between invisible snares.

'Watch out!' barked Benbow. But Wilf had already reached Garracker, pulled his knife out, and was hacking at the taut rope that ran from the ground to a tether high on the wall.

'Get ready!' he cried. An instant later Garracker came reeling down in a headlong rush, hit the ground and lay still.

Wilf bent over him anxiously. 'Are you hurt? I'll just get this rope off your leg.' He sawed at the loop, until Garracker sat up and pushed him roughly away.

'Leave it!' he shouted. The only thing that seemed to be hurt was his pride. 'Stop crawling all over me! Benbow! Come and get this hideous brat off me!' Wilf flinched away. '*Benbow!* For crying out loud! Is this City full of idiots?'

'Only the one sitting in front of me,' growled Benbow.

'*What?*'

Benbow's heart was thumping in fury. 'You're in Dowie's territory.'

'Then get me out of it, damn you!' yelled Garracker. 'I've had enough of this infernal stinking City! As soon as I've found all my clones, I'm going to raze it to the ground!'

'You're going to *what?*' Benbow went rigid.

'I'm going to flatten this blasted City, just like I planned all along. I only put my plans on hold while you found the clones! I told Dowie – and look at the thanks I get!' Garracker scrambled to his feet and bellowed furiously into the darkness. 'Hear me, Dowie? I'll tear this place down, whether you like it or not! Starting with the Town Hall!'

'You *can't*,' said Benbow thickly, his human voice almost failing him.

'Who's going to stop me?'

Benbow was aghast. His City, lost forever! Yet he should have known Garracker always meant to destroy it. He shook his head, ashamed of his stupidity.

'Don't just stand there! Get me out of here, Benbow!' snarled Garracker.

Benbow paused. Loyalty was everything to him. It was his job, his instinct, and his pride. But loyalty to Garracker...? Why should he obey this monstrous human? Why couldn't he just abandon Garracker, and let the City swallow him whole?

'Be loyal to the City,' he murmured. But what City? What would be left, at the end of all this?

'Get a move on, damn you!' yelled Garracker.

Numbly, Benbow barked his orders to the dogs. He told McCool to take the children home, for he wanted Wilf out of Garracker's sight.

Then, with the two other dogs, he escorted Garracker and Slane through the silent midnight streets. He sensed a hundred unseen watchers in the dark, and wondered why no one accosted them. But the gangs were either too afraid of Garracker – who swore continually under his breath – or too glad to see the back of Slane, who yowled like a cat, singing tunelessly in his one-man language.

'Benbow,' breathed Daffodil through the yowling, as at last they crossed the wasteland to the Fringes, 'what will Garracker do with him?'

Benbow glanced at Garracker, gripping Slane's shoulder in an iron hand, his face set hard. Slane twisted in his grasp, as slippery as a fish.

Worlds apart, thought Benbow, and a chill ran through him.

'I don't know,' he answered to the night. 'And I don't want to know.'

Chapter Nineteen

'You've put an end to the fires. That's good, isn't it?'

'Yes,' said Benbow shortly.

'And after all, something had to be done with Slane.'

'I suppose.'

'If Slane wasn't with Garracker, he'd just be sent to a secure Home,' said Elise consolingly. 'Even Garracker can't be worse than *that*.'

'He'll probably end up in a Home anyway,' growled Benbow, 'as soon as Garracker loses patience with him. Either that, or he'll have an accident.'

'What are you saying?'

'Nothing.' He sighed deeply. 'I'm tired, that's all.'

'Then rest,' said Elise.

Since Tonto lay smugly in Benbow's basket, Benbow flopped onto the floor. McCool sprawled at his side, and Daffodil lay at his tail. Junior and Elise completed the circle round the stove: already half-asleep, their eyes were dark liquid glints beneath low lids. Only Araby sat aloof and apart. The sounds of dogs coughing and snoring came from the other dormitory.

Benbow shifted restlessly. 'I don't know what to do.'

'What d'you mean?' asked Junior drowsily.

'I don't want to be at Garracker's beck and call. But what can I do? Should I resign? What future is there for a three-legged police dog?'

'If you resign, then we all do,' said Daffodil loyally.

'Speak for yourself,' grunted Araby.

'I don't want you to resign,' said Elise, her breath rasping in her chest. 'I'm retiring soon. You'll be needed at the Station.'

'I'm not indispensable,' said Benbow. 'There are plenty of others to take my place.' He glanced round at his clones, suddenly feeling a great loneliness. Outwardly, they were *him*. But inwardly? They couldn't share his thoughts or memories. How could they understand him?

'I don't want to find the third clone,' he said miserably. 'Three Garrackers are enough. And whether we find him or not, Garracker's going to destroy the City anyway. There's no happy ending, whatever I do.'

'Then don't worry about it,' yawned McCool. 'What happens, happens.'

Elise laid her grey muzzle close to his. 'Sleep, Benbow.'

Benbow sighed and eased off his plastic leg. His bruises kept him awake for some time; and when at last he slept, he dreamt of rats. He often did, after rat for tea – rats nipped and scurried through his dreams. But this time, the rats were fleeing headlong with the clatter of a thousand tiny claws, flowing through the streets in a grey flood.

Benbow dreamt he sat under the Hopeful Insurance Building, at the City's edge, and watched the rats pour out across the Fringes. And then, in quite a leisurely way, the City began to fall. Top floors broke free of their towers and floated lazily to the ground. Buildings drifted downwards to land with a gentle, soundless crash.

'The children!' thought Benbow in his dream. He tried to catch them as they toppled from the rope-walks, but his legs were paralysed. Children and dogs rained down upon him, as the City collapsed. They lay in a great crying, howling pile in the middle of the Recycler's yard. And then there was nothing but rubble and a huge, white, dusty sky.

Benbow woke, gasping. He was filled with a desperate sadness, but at least he knew now what to do. He scrambled to his feet, clumsy with sleep. A pale dawn was filtering through the window.

'Up! Up!' barked Benbow urgently, and the other dogs raised their heads in drowsy bewilderment.

'What is it?'

'Get up! Get moving! No time to waste! I need the City all together, *now*!'

'He's gone crazy,' purred Tonto.

'You're still asleep, Benbow!' growled Araby. 'You're dreaming!'

'I'm not. Wake up!'

'Certainly not,' said Tonto. 'This is far too comfortable a basket, although I have to say it smells disgusting. No offence.' He snuggled down again.

Benbow struggled to put on his leg, failed, picked it up in his mouth and hurried to the other dormitory where Natty and Wilf slept in a sprawl of dogs. The room stank of damp dog and Wilf's ointment.

'Strap it on for me,' barked Benbow, dropping the leg on Natty, who was wrapped in a huddle of old blankets.

She sat up, rubbing her eyes. There was a moan from

beneath the bedclothes, and an arm emerged. Benbow saw a red, puckered shoulder, and as the blankets slipped away, a bare, stretched scalp.

Benbow leapt backwards. 'Where's his *hair*?' he barked in startled Dog. Who was this bald child? But it was Wilf, after all, who started up in a flurry of bedclothes, staring at him with one good eye and one twisted eyelid. Seeing Benbow, he yanked a handful of red hair from under his pillow and jammed it on his head. Then, pulling out his eye-patch, he put it on with an unsteady hand.

'Sorry,' said Benbow sheepishly, in Human. 'Thought you were someone else. Didn't know it was a wig.'

Natty began to strap on Benbow's leg, a little roughly.

'All the dogs in here are used to him,' she said.

'Yes, of course.' Embarrassed, Benbow ducked his head at the waking dogs, who were looking curious. 'Sorry. I'm still a stranger here. The hair's very convincing.'

'It's *my* hair,' said Natty. 'I cut my hair and made that wig for Wilf, until his own grows back.'

'It won't grow back,' said Wilf, 'any more than my eye will, or Benbow's leg.'

'It's better than it used to be,' said Natty.

'Because she keeps on at me,' said Wilf mildly, 'wash and ointment, every day.'

Benbow nosed gently at the red wig and licked the bad side of Wilf's face with affectionate apology. It tasted of hospital.

Then he turned to face the dogs. 'I want a message sent throughout the City. Tell *everyone* to come to the

Recycler's yard at mid-day. That's everyone – all the gangs, big and small, dogs and children.'

'What for?' asked Wilf.

'I want to talk to the whole City together. People won't come to the Station, but the yard is big, and it's neutral territory. You two had better go and warn the Recycler that the City is about to descend on her.'

'Doesn't she know?'

'Not yet.'

'She'll hate it,' said Wilf, grinning.

Chapter Twenty

'I hate this,' said the Recycler. 'I don't like *people*. I stayed in the City to get away from *people*.'

Benbow gazed around the yard. Children were perched on every mound of junk, knees pulled up to chins, their scrawny dogs beside them... Over a thousand, he guessed, child and dog.

Daffodil asked diffidently, 'Who are you, Recycler?'

At first it seemed she wouldn't answer, but then she muttered, 'I was the College Caretaker. When it closed, I couldn't bear to leave. I hid in the College until the first gangs moved in, and kicked me out. But I waited. They left, in the end, and I came back. Lovely and peaceful it was then. Not a soul.'

'But where did you get all your things?'

'The gangs burnt out the College, made a terrible mess. Well, you can see.' She nodded at the ruined walls. 'I started to collect stuff to repair it, but the job was too big for me. Anyway, no one wanted the College any more. They wanted my things though. So I started selling 'em. Didn't bargain for this, though.' She glared around the yard. 'Did you have to ask everyone?'

'Everyone,' said Benbow, scanning the crowd. He saw quick-tempered Greenspan, biting his nails amidst his gang, and Dowie, with Trugg and Camilla. Opposite them sat Nile, surrounded by helmeted Warriors; and there was Angel, her cloud of hair lifting about her head, and her sisters beside her.

Benbow trotted over hopefully, with the pups pattering after him.

'Hello, Angel.'

'Go away, clone,' said Angel coldly, turning to her sister.

Benbow's heart sank. But Daffodil, tail wagging, said, '*He's* not a clone. *I* am.'

'You're all clones, as far as I'm concerned,' said Angel. 'All unnatural. Before we know it, the City could be overrun with Benbows.' Daffodil's tail stopped wagging.

'Nice idea,' said McCool. 'How about being overrun with Angels?' He looked at her sisters. 'Never heard of identical twins?'

'Twins are different,' said Angel.

'So are we,' said McCool.

'It's not our fault!' burst out Daffodil. 'You can't blame us for being born, only for what we do afterwards! Not that we've done anything yet, and anyway, I'm proud to be made of the Admiral's leg, and so would you be—' Daffodil floundered to a standstill.

McCool said, 'What he means is, you are what you are. Y'know?'

'No,' said Angel. 'Why did you call us here, Benbow?'

But Benbow moved away. He couldn't speak to her. Instead, sick at heart, he barked to the crowd for silence. As the chatter subsided, he addressed them in his clearest Human.

'Thank you for coming,' he began. 'This is the first

time everyone in the City has met together. It's never happened before. Until now, we've gone our separate ways: we've been busy patrolling, and you, surviving. But things are changing in the City. Soon, no one will survive here any longer – if Garracker has his way.'

The crowd murmured, as if in recognition of something they had long feared.

'Why now?' barked a Rottweiler.

'I'll explain.' Taking a deep breath, Benbow related the events of the past few weeks in alternate Human and Dog. The crowd listened intently as he told them about Garracker's cloning and its consequences, the finding of Dowie, and of Slane.

'Dowie? Slane?' cried Angel incredulously. 'They're clones?' She stared at Dowie. 'You're *Garracker*.'

'No, I'm not!' protested Dowie. 'I'm nothing like him! All right, we both like to make things work, we get things done. But *I'm not him*. He has no friends, just men who agree with everything he says. He doesn't even keep a dog!' Trugg gave a short, appalled bark.

'But if you're his clone,' said Angel. She didn't finish her sentence, but sat staring into space.

'Why are you telling us this?' asked Greenspan.

Benbow answered. 'As soon as Garracker finds the third clone, he intends to destroy the City.'

Dowie leapt furiously from his seat. 'I won't let him! I'll blow up his machines before he can lay a finger on our City!'

'We'll fight him to the death!' One of the Western Warriors jumped to his feet, waving a rusty iron bar.

Tomahawk, thought Benbow with vexation, as he barked a fierce reproof.

'Fight Garracker? He can buy explosives by the ton, and hire an army that would annihilate you Warriors! Don't even think about it!'

'Then what are we supposed to do?' asked Nile sullenly.

Benbow hesitated, for he knew his audience would not like the answer. He growled the words deep in his throat.

'You have to leave. Every girl, boy and dog. You all have to leave the City. There's no other way.' He waited for the protest; and it came, in a swelling wave of barks and shouts. Benbow raised his voice. 'If you leave now, you'll be safe. We'll find you all homes Outside. You'll have food, warmth, schools—' But the surge of angry voices drowned him out.

'I'm not going into a home!' yelled Dowie. 'I'm my own master!'

'That's right! We're all our own masters here!' yelped a terrier.

'We'll fight for our freedom!' shouted Tomahawk.

'You police dogs have always wanted us out,' cried Greenspan. 'Always been trying to force us to go!'

'That's not true!' protested Benbow. 'We've given you the chance, if you wished.' Even now, he saw some wistful faces in the crowd: children who longed for homes Outside, he guessed, but were afraid to ask.

'I don't want to leave either,' he declared, 'but it's the only sensible course to take. Life Outside will be better than you think. You'll have proper meals, no more rat, a family—'

'Stop! Don't listen! It's all lies!'

It was a weak voice, cracking hoarsely, yet everyone fell silent as the speaker hobbled forward: a thin, pale boy, unknown to Benbow, and leaning heavily on crutches.

'Don't listen!' he said. 'I've tried it. I've been in a Home. A Home with a capital H.' There was a sharp intake of breath from the crowd. Children who got put in Homes seldom came back.

'Who are you?' demanded Benbow.

The boy gazed at him bleakly. 'I'm vermin. Scum. Not worth a name.'

But the Recycler whispered incredulously, 'Carlo?' and sat down heavily on a pile of planks. '*Carlo . . .*' Then Benbow remembered her litany of children. Carlo: taken Out to hospital, never seen again . . .

Carlo regarded her with cold, accusing eyes. 'You never came to get me,' he said. 'Too busy with your things, I expect.'

'They wouldn't have let me bring you back,' said the Recycler, looking suddenly much smaller and older.

'They put me in a Home while my leg was still in plaster,' said Carlo. 'The kids beat me up and stole my crutches. My leg's never healed properly. They stole my food as well. You know what they called me? City scum. Rat-boy. Dirt-brain. Homes? *Pah!*' He spat.

'No! That's not right,' cried Benbow, horrified. 'Homes aren't like that!' *Could* they be? His brain whirled. He knew no dog would treat another dog that way.

Carlo laughed hollowly. 'How would you know?'

Benbow was bewildered and speechless. But Araby came to his rescue.

'You were unlucky. Foster homes are quite different,' he said. 'They're with real families. I've been in one, and they were good to me!'

'You're a dog,' said Carlo bitterly. 'Not a child. We're not wanted. Nobody likes City children. We're just freaks, filthy rat-eaters. First chance to escape, I took it.'

Benbow felt as if the world had suddenly turned dark and strange. All those children he had persuaded to abandon the City... surely they were happy? Surely they would have come back otherwise? But he knew little of the world Outside.

Araby, at least, could still speak confidently. 'If you go Outside, it need not be for long. Garracker will rebuild the City. New houses – schools – hostels – who knows?'

But Dowie smiled grimly. 'Garracker's not interested in homeless children. He wants new office blocks full of businessmen making money. Maybe an art gallery as a monument to himself. The Garracker Gallery! He'd like that.' His smile twisted.

Araby sighed. 'It seems to me this City could do with some change: fewer rats, for instance, and a proper water supply. As far as I can see, it's hell on earth.'

'It's the hell they know,' said Benbow softly. He understood how they felt. This was his City, too. Its tangled smells and rotting towers and dark corners were a part of him. To lose the City would be worse than losing his leg. Yet he also knew that the City was a dreadful place.

'Don't leave! Don't go Outside!' cried Carlo harshly. 'There's nothing for you there!' And looking at the children's fearful faces, Benbow knew that he would never persuade them to leave the City now. His great plan had failed.

Chapter Twenty-one

'They won't go,' he said, despairing. 'It'll be too late to save them, once the bulldozers move in. If they try to stay in the towers, they'll be killed—'

Daffodil licked him consolingly. 'You did your best, Admiral!'

'Not good enough,' groaned Benbow. His tail drooped, as he heard Angel's voice ring out above the crowd.

'What about Garracker's clones?' she cried. 'He's gone to all this trouble to track them down – surely he'll listen to their wishes? Can't Dowie persuade Garracker to leave the City alone?'

'Hah! He won't listen to *me*,' said Dowie. 'We've fallen out. And you can forget about Slane: he's a disaster area.'

The children fell quiet, looking at Dowie and thinking of his mirror image, Slane, a boy back to front and wrong way round, neglected even by the City, with no Recycler to house him, no gang to protect him, no dog to befriend him, no companions but the skulking cats.

'What about this third clone, then?' demanded Greenspan. 'Maybe he could persuade Garracker. Or we could use him to hold Garracker to ransom!'

'There is no third clone,' said Dowie. 'The third clone is dead.'

'How can we be sure?'

For answer, Dowie strode forward. 'Well?' he demanded. 'Seen anyone like me around? The whole City's here. Is one of you my twin?'

The children twisted round to scan each others' faces. The disappointed murmurs came floating back: 'Not here . . . No.' But Benbow noticed that Angel's gang were watching *her*. Slowly, Angel shook her head.

'There is no third clone,' repeated Dowie firmly.

'Isn't there?' Benbow's eyes narrowed. The Western Warriors were still wearing their helmets, whose angry grey stink disguised their true scent. 'We haven't seen all the faces yet,' he growled.

Dowie followed his gaze, and laughed derisively. 'That mob? That's only Nile and his lot in fancy dress.'

'Nevertheless. Warriors, take off your helmets!' Benbow barked.

'We are the Western Warriors, and we don't obey anyone but our General!' shouted Tomahawk. 'We'll fight you first!'

Benbow rumbled in exasperation. 'Then, *General*, please remove your helmet, and order your warriors to do likewise.'

'Won't,' said Nile.

'Oh, I think you should,' said McCool. 'You're meant to be all brothers in the City. And look at you, playing at little soldiers, and messing everyone around. Let's see your faces!'

'No,' said Nile uncertainly.

'Want a *real* fight?' asked McCool, his voice low and level. 'I'll give you a *real* fight.' His hackles rose, his tail stiffened, and his lip curled back to show his snarling teeth. Benbow realised with a shock that McCool was not a dog he'd want to tangle with. Nile evidently felt the same way, for he took a step back. McCool took a step forward.

Nile's panicky voice shrieked out. 'All right! All right! Warriors – take off your helmets!'

The Warriors looked at the dogs, and their trembling General, and one by one obeyed. As the helmets thudded to the ground, Benbow scanned each grimy, sullen face. None of them looked anything like Dowie. At last the only one still helmeted was Tomahawk.

'You too,' growled McCool.

'I'm keeping my helmet!' yelled Tomahawk. 'You're all cowards. I'll fight for my City. I'll fight Garracker!' He swung the metal bar around his head until it sang.

'Put that down!' commanded Benbow. 'You can't fight Garracker!'

'We can if we've got weapons!'

'What, sticks and stones?'

'There are guns in the College,' shouted Tomahawk. 'We can fight Garracker with guns! Come on, Warriors – let's go in and get 'em!'

Sprinting suddenly past the startled dogs, Tomahawk disappeared through the College doorway. Some of the other Warriors began to follow, but McCool leapt in front of them, snarling.

'Guns? They mustn't get hold of *guns*!' barked Araby, and he dashed into the College after Tomahawk. The other dogs ran to help McCool, snapping and growling at the Warriors until they retreated in a cowering huddle.

'*Guns?*' repeated Benbow in alarm. 'That's not true, is it, Recycler?'

'Afraid so,' said the Recycler tightly. 'The old gang years ago left them behind. I never knew what to do with 'em. One of my children joined Nile's gang; he must have told 'em.'

Benbow's head reeled at the thought of guns in the City. 'But if Tomahawk gets hold of them—'

'Benbow!' cried Angel. 'Look up there!'

High on the ruined College walls climbed Tomahawk. Balancing precariously on the crumbling brick, he held something long in his hand. A shotgun... Then Araby came into sight, scrambling over the ragged wall behind him. Benbow held his breath. They were a long way up.

'Stop! You're under arrest!' barked Araby. 'Drop the gun!'

'Don't try and get me, or I'll shoot you!' shouted Tomahawk.

'Oh, be careful, Araby!' cried Daffodil. 'Don't look down!'

High on his jagged perch, Araby looked down – and froze. Benbow saw his ears lie back, and his body begin to shudder. His bark died to a whimper, as he slowly crouched back on his haunches.

Tomahawk yelled triumphantly. 'Yah! Get down, dog! Do as I say, *dog*!'

Brandishing the gun, he leapt wildly at Araby. But as he landed on the ruined wall, it broke beneath his feet.

Bricks tumbled to the ground below, scattering children in all directions.

Tomahawk nearly fell along with the bricks. He lost his footing, dropped the gun and collapsed on his stomach with a surprised grunt. The shotgun flew through the air, turning lazily, and landed harmlessly near Benbow. Half-lying on the wall, feet dangling, Tomahawk clung on with his arms while his legs flailed helplessly for a foothold.

'Help!' he wailed. '*Help me!*' But Araby still crouched motionless.

'I'm going up after them!' cried McCool, and he raced into the College. Benbow stared upwards, afraid to bark in case he startled them and made things worse.

'Keep calm, Araby,' he whispered. All around him, dogs were whimpering in fear. One set up a mournful howl in accompaniment to Tomahawk's frantic bellows.

'Help me! Get me *down*!'

Then Araby's twitching muscles bunched. Slowly, he began to move. Crouching on the wall's edge, he started to creep towards the shrieking Tomahawk. More lumps of brick rattled down as Araby reached the floundering child, and leaned over to grasp his collar in his teeth. Tomahawk grabbed frenziedly at Araby's coat, almost yanking him over the edge.

'He's too heavy for Araby!' cried Daffodil. 'They're both going to die!'

Benbow saw Araby wince and brace his legs. Despite his strength, he was being gradually dragged closer and closer to the edge – yet still he clung on grimly to Tomahawk's collar. Benbow felt as if the world had gone into slow motion. How long before McCool reached them? Another brick plunged down, and Tomahawk cried out. Araby slipped further forward.

'He'll fall!' cried Natty, her hands at her mouth.

But Araby didn't fall.

He jumped.

Chapter Twenty-two

He sprang out in a great arc from the crumbling wall, taking Tomahawk with him. Tomahawk's shriek echoed through the air.

Benbow closed his eyes. This was worse than his dream. He couldn't bear to see the tumbling bodies land. He prayed that time might stop, that it might never happen.

But he could not shut out the children's screams. Nor the thud; nor the gasp; nor the silence.

Benbow opened his eyes. Araby and Tomahawk lay huddled on top of the heap of tyres. There was a groan. A tyre moved; Tomahawk sat up, and fell back again.

Benbow ran over and tried, unsuccessfully, to clamber up the pile. Natty and Wilf scrambled past him to reach the fallen pair. They pulled at Tomahawk, who groaned again, rolled over and slithered down to land at Benbow's feet.

The broken helmet fell away, and Benbow saw that Tomahawk could never have been the third clone. Wrong sex, for a start.

It didn't seem to matter now. The children had reached Araby, and were trying to move him.

'Careful,' said Benbow huskily, as Araby's limp body came sliding down the tyres and lay still.

'Araby?' Benbow bent over him. For an agonising

moment, he could not tell if Araby was breathing. Then he saw the young dog's chest heave, and an eyelid flicker. As Benbow gently licked his coat, Araby murmured something, as if in sleep.

'What's that?' Benbow put his ear close to Araby's mouth.

'Thought they were *bouncy*,' muttered Araby.

Natty tumbled down the heap of tyres and knelt by Araby to run a practised hand over his body and legs. 'I can't feel anything broken,' she said. 'But he may have cracked a rib or two. No, Araby, don't try to sit up!'

'Tomahawk all right?' Araby whispered.

'She's fine.' Benbow licked his ear. 'When I told you to practise heights, that wasn't quite what I meant.'

'Bit drastic,' murmured Araby.

Benbow straightened up. Relief made him suddenly angry, and he turned on Tomahawk.

'Idiot!' he barked. 'You and your guns! You nearly got yourself killed!'

'I hurt all over,' moaned Tomahawk, sitting up and dolefully shaking each limb in turn.

'You're lucky to be alive!' snapped Benbow. 'Why couldn't you just take off that stupid helmet?'

'Don't want to be a girl,' muttered Tomahawk. 'Want to be a Warrior.'

'I'll tolerate no Warriors in my City. The Western Warriors are disbanded – as from now! Get out of here!'

'Can't move,' grumbled Tomahawk. 'Why should I?'

The Recycler bent down to her. Her voice was as thin and sharp as a needle.

'Because I say so,' she said. 'Not just the Warriors.' Straightening up, she fixed the crowd with a piercing glare. 'I've had enough. I want *everybody* out of my yard. *Now*. Well? What are you waiting for?'

Tomahawk stumbled to her feet. The children slowly climbed down off their perches, and the dogs stood up and shook themselves sheepishly.

'*All of you.*' The Recycler stared at them icily until they began to shuffle towards the gate. Her face twisted for a moment. 'Except you, Carlo. You don't have to go.'

'I do,' said Carlo distantly, picking up his crutches.

'Hang on, Recycler— ' began Dowie.

'Didn't you hear me? I own this place, and I said GO.'

She looked less like a sparrow now than a hawk, glaring at him with a pitiless eye. Dowie dropped his gaze and began to follow the crowd trailing towards the gate.

'You're not the owner, you're the caretaker,' said Wilf boldly, to Benbow's surprise.

'Go,' repeated the Recycler.

'Well, you are,' said Wilf as he ran out. 'It's not the same thing at all.'

Araby got shakily to his feet. McCool and Junior hurried to support him as he began to walk, staggering a little. Benbow followed with head bowed.

'Wait,' said the Recycler.

He stopped.

'*You*,' she said. 'Nile. You look like a strong boy. You can stay and help me clear up this mess. Well? Didn't you hear me?' For Nile was standing dumbstruck. 'Pick up those tyres, and put them back on the pile. Neatly!'

Flustered, Nile lifted up a tyre. The rest of the City's inhabitants slunk out of the yard. Last of all was Benbow, tail between his legs.

Everything had gone wrong, he thought. His dream had nearly become a nightmare. He had achieved nothing.

Or almost nothing . . .

Chapter Twenty-three

For Angel was waiting for him.

In the chill shadow outside the College wall, she said quietly, 'Benbow.'

He stopped. Slowly she walked over to him, running a finger along the crumbling wall.

'I'll be leaving the City soon.'

'Why?' said Benbow. Something inside him was hurting.

'I'm getting old. I must be nearly sixteen... I want something else. I want – oh – soft beds, and warmth, and shops, and food that isn't stolen. And I want to see, to learn.'

'Do you want me to find you a home?' asked Benbow dully.

'No. I'll find my own. I need to go, Benbow. But I still care about the City.' She pulled a flake of brick from the wall. Benbow watched it float to the ground.

'I didn't understand,' said Angel quietly. 'I thought your clones were you, multiplied, like some vile magic trick. I didn't realise, until I heard them talk... and then I learnt that Dowie is one too... and so... '

She paused. Benbow waited.

'And so I want to give you something.'

'What is it?' Benbow's tail began to wag, unstoppably, by instinct.

'It's this.' She knelt beside him, put her thin arms round his neck and hugged him: then kissed his forehead and said, in a whispered breath, 'Wilf is the third clone.'

Benbow's tail stopped wagging. '*Wilf?*'

'You know he used to be in my gang? Ten years ago it wasn't my gang, of course, but I remember them finding Wilf and Natty, and Natty's older sister, who was sick. We took them in. But Wilf wasn't their brother at all.'

'What?' Benbow couldn't grasp it.

'Natty always claimed Wilf was her brother. But her sister told me he wasn't really, they just found him somewhere. I didn't think it mattered – thought he was just another City stray, until I first saw Dowie and realised how alike they looked. I knew they must be related, brothers or cousins maybe. But it didn't seem important then.'

'Does Dowie know?' asked Benbow sharply.

'No. He never met Wilf – not before the accident, anyway; and Wilf looks quite different now.'

Benbow tried to gather his thoughts. He felt as though the City he knew was shattering into a thousand flying fragments. Wilf – the third clone? How could he have missed it? Why had he not scented it? But he'd never seen deeper than Wilf's scars, nor smelt further than his ointment.

'Does anyone else know?' he asked hoarsely.

'Some of my gang. I told them to say nothing. No one else – Wilf always kept himself to himself. He liked solitude better than company.'

Benbow thought of Slane.

'He's always been quiet, has Wilf,' said Angel, 'though not so quiet as he is now. He's lucky he's had Natty to protect him.'

'He is.' Something else occurred to Benbow. 'Does *he* know?'

'I'm certain he doesn't,' said Angel. She smiled wryly. 'Not many mirrors in the City. I doubt if he's ever seen his own reflection. But Natty must have realised. And I think you need to know it too.' She stroked Benbow's ears gently. 'Goodbye, Benbow, old friend. My sister Rose will take over when I've gone.'

'Goodbye, Angel.' There was a hollow space in Benbow's stomach. He watched her walk away, then trudged slowly back to where Daffodil was waiting patiently.

'Are you all right, Ad – Benbow?'

'Fine.'

'You're sad.'

'Yes. Angel's leaving.' Though half his sadness was for Wilf.

Daffodil gave him a quick, diffident lick. 'Don't worry! You've still got us. Though we're not much use yet…'

'You're improving,' said Benbow, and licked him back. He found a comfortable companionship in walking home with Daffodil, as if he were a younger brother.

Back at the Station, they found Araby lying quietly, at Natty's insistence, in Benbow's basket. Daffodil immediately began to fuss over him, offering him bones, and licks, and water, and for once Araby didn't snap back.

Benbow went in search of Natty. She was in the outhouse with Wilf, washing the dog-blankets.

'We're getting low on rats, Wilf,' said Benbow. 'How are your traps doing?'

Wilf smiled. 'I'll go and check!' He dropped the soap and hurried out eagerly. Benbow was left alone with Natty, nervously dipping a wet blanket in and out of the tub. She looked at him sidelong.

'I know about Wilf,' said Benbow. 'Angel told me.'

'I thought she might.' Natty sounded choked. 'But he *is* my brother! He's always been my brother, ever since I found him!'

'When was that?' asked Benbow gently.

'He was just a baby, and I was only three or four... I was with my big sister Jo and our dog, Brewer. We were out one day, hunting rats, and I remember hearing this funny little mewing noise inside a building... So I went in, and there was a baby sitting in the middle of the floor, playing with a piece of wood.'

'Just one baby?'

'Yes. Almost a toddler. He tried to stand up, but he couldn't. So I picked him up and cuddled him – I could just lift him – and he was so warm and soft and wriggly and he gurgled like a drain.' A tear ran down Natty's cheek. 'He was so funny. Jo said we could keep him if nobody else claimed him, and he's been my brother ever since. We caught hundreds of rats and sold them to the Recycler in exchange for milk. Then Jo got sick, and couldn't get up—'

'And Angel's gang found you.'

'Yes. They carried Jo Outside to a hospital, and they took me and Wilf into the gang. He's always been mine!' implored Natty.

'You've always cared for him,' said Benbow gently. 'But he doesn't belong to anyone.'

Natty wiped her eyes furiously. 'I thought he'd died in that fire. When you brought him out, I felt turned to stone because I thought he was dead. They took him away, and I had to hunt him down in hospital. Nobody told me where he was, but I found him. They were going to put him in a Home. But I got him back.'

'And brought him to live at the Station.'

'He wanted to be near you,' said Natty, 'and it seemed so important to him that I decided to ask at the Station for a job. He's been happy here. Even happier, the last week or two. I've seen the difference. He likes all the dogs, you know – but one of you, in particular, is very special to him.'

'Ah,' said Benbow.

'Yes. He loves McCool,' said Natty.

'Oh,' said Benbow.

'I don't want to give him up! He mustn't go to Garracker!' cried Natty passionately. 'He'd hate it! You've seen how cruel Garracker is. He mustn't go!'

'Hush, Natty,' said Benbow, for she was shouting, and he was worried that someone would overhear. Natty blew her nose on the blanket, and dropped it back in the bucket, sniffing.

'Wilf doesn't know?' asked Benbow.

'I haven't told him. I knew as soon as I saw Dowie, in

the Town Hall that day the ceiling collapsed – he had Wilf's old face. It gave me a terrible shock. But Wilf?' She shook her head. 'He has no idea that he's the third clone.'

'I do now,' said Wilf. He stepped through the door and flung a dead rat into the corner.

'Wilf!' Natty looked aghast.

Wilf slumped to the floor. Drawing up his legs, he sat huddled, face buried on his knees.

'I thought I was just me,' he mumbled, 'and now I'm Dowie, and Slane, and Garracker. I don't want to be any of them.'

Natty knelt and hugged him. 'You're still Wilf! Nothing's changed.'

'Everything's changed,' said Wilf, his voice remote. 'Now I've got to go to Garracker, and persuade him to save the City.'

'No! You don't need to do anything!'

'I do.' Wilf looked up. His face was even more like a mask than usual. 'Garracker's waiting for me. I have to go and meet my maker.'

Chapter Twenty-four

'I'm not handing Wilf over,' said Benbow. 'Not Wilf. Not to Garracker.' It was a new, odd feeling, this disobedience; as if a rope-walk had collapsed beneath him and left him running through the air.

'Your decision,' said Elise.

'He's right. No point handing Wilf over. Garracker's going to knock the City down anyway,' said McCool.

'Maybe we could just tell him that the third clone exists?' suggested Daffodil. 'He wouldn't destroy the City if his clone's still hidden in it.'

'He'd want proof,' pointed out Elise.

'We could give Garracker something he could test, like hair.' Benbow remembered too late. 'Or nail clippings.'

'He'd say they were Dowie's,' said Araby. 'He'd want to see Wilf in the flesh.'

And there they paused. Garracker *had* seen Wilf in the flesh. What if he didn't want this clone, with its ruined face and eye-patch? Benbow thought it all too likely. Two damaged clones – first Slane, now Wilf – might be too much for Garracker to take.

'Do nothing yet. Just wait,' advised Elise.

'Wait for what?' growled Benbow. 'Wait for Garracker to send in his army?' Yet he could think of nothing else to do: so he waited.

Several days passed, turning to a week, then two; and

although Benbow's ears were constantly pricked for the roar of tanks, all remained quiet. Wilf stayed at the Station. The dogs went back on patrol. Araby soon recovered from his fall, and was able to join them.

These days, since the gathering in the Recycler's yard, more children came out to talk to the patrolling dogs, or just to say hello. Voices sang down from the rope-walks:

'Morning Benbow Daffodil McCool and Ara-*beee*!' for suddenly everyone knew their names. Daffodil loved this. Araby didn't mind it as much as Benbow expected, but McCool obviously hated it. He cringed when his name was called.

'What's the problem?' Benbow asked him one morning. He fell back alongside McCool, the clone he felt he knew least well. For McCool was often absent from the Station, away exploring: nosing down secret alleys and poking into forgotten corners, sliding into conversations with strange dogs in which he seemed to learn a lot whilst saying very little.

He said little at the Station either. Whilst Daffodil was growing in confidence, and Araby was slowly unbending, McCool seemed to have got quieter. It worried Benbow.

'What's the problem?' he repeated, softly so the others wouldn't hear.

'Nothing,' said McCool. Two children sidled out of a doorway, plainly wanting a word. Araby addressed the older in a business-like way whilst Daffodil romped with the younger, who smiled and stroked him.

But McCool drifted away, peered through a dark

window, gazed longingly down a silent passage. Benbow limped after him.

'Aren't you happy here?' he asked.

McCool shrugged. 'It's all right. The City's interesting. But I feel like the Recycler: too many people around. Rather be off on my own.'

'Yes, I'd noticed,' said Benbow.

'I'm not so good in a team,' said McCool apologetically. 'I think better by myself.'

'You don't care for going on patrol,' said Benbow.

McCool's tail slumped. 'I know I *should*. Think something must have gone wrong with my genes. All this walking around, taking names, noting crimes just bores me. Sorry.'

Benbow sympathised. He found patrols tedious too, and felt the pull of the City's darkness and strangeness, its silent chasms full of secrets.

'You might be happier training for undercover work,' he said thoughtfully. 'Tracking down criminals who sneak into the City... That's what I used to do.'

'Really?'

'Before my leg stopped me. I enjoyed it. I think you might be good at it.'

'Undercover...' McCool fell silent. After a moment, his tail perked up a little. 'Wouldn't mind that,' he said.

Araby cantered over. 'Two more who want to leave!' he reported. 'I've told them to come to the Station tomorrow.'

'I hope we can get them a really good home Outside,' said Daffodil. 'I've promised to visit that little girl to make sure she's all right.'

Benbow nodded. That made fourteen chil... had approached them, wanting to start a new... Outside, despite Carlo's warnings. Benbow was determined to run checks on their homes, make sure they were happy... But most children were opting to stay in the City, no matter what Garracker might do; and Benbow knew that Garracker would do something, soon. Fourteen wasn't enough.

'Lunchtime,' he said, feeling depressed. Even the thought of rat and bacon pie failed to console him as he trudged towards the Station.

Halfway home, the dogs all halted, ears twitching, listening intently. They looked at each other.

'Coming this way,' said McCool.

'Four of them,' added Daffodil, whom Benbow suspected of having the sharpest ears of the lot.

'Tanks?' guessed Araby.

'No... Different engine note. Tractors, maybe.'

'We'd better investigate,' said Benbow, reluctantly. He wanted his lunch.

The distant rumble was heading for the heart of the City. The pups raced away, not bothering to wait for Benbow. Hardly pups any more, he thought; they were nearly full-grown now. No chance of keeping up with them. As he struggled through the littered streets, he cursed his leg automatically – then realised he didn't mean it. Something had shifted in his world. He was used to his plastic leg: it had become part of him.

At Empire Row the young dogs halted, their bodies expressing alarm. On the horizon loomed four monsters:

crane, digger, bulldozer, truck... They heaved and pitched over the rubble like warships over a petrified sea.

The invasion at last, thought Benbow.

Led by the bulldozer, the machines turned towards the Museum. Without even slowing, they charged at the Museum wall, through the ragged hole left by Garracker's tank. It sounded as if the whole City was exploding. The wall disappeared in a fountain of flying stone.

The dogs approached cautiously as the machines thundered into the Museum. Only the crane stayed outside. Children appeared, attracted by the noise, and trickling up to the Museum, pooled there to watch, with a horde of interested dogs. Wilf and Natty came running to join them; and then Dowie arrived.

Dowie was furious. He marched to the Museum with Trugg at his heels, stood in the gap, arms akimbo, and yelled,

'Garracker? What the devil do you think you're doing? Get your machines out of my City!'

Garracker jumped down from the bulldozer's cab. He looked different: strange, and smaller, in dirty, creased blue overalls.

'Go away,' he said. 'I'm busy.'

'Is that any way to talk to your clone and heir?' jeered Dowie.

'I've disowned you, Dowie. You're nothing to me.'

'I'm everything! I'm *you*! You can't disown me!'

But Garracker had turned his back. 'Go away.' He sounded distracted, as if he really didn't care what Dowie said.

Dowie spun on his heel, face dark as a storm. 'Hear that?' He scowled at Benbow. 'Thinks I'm nothing, does he? How dare he!'

'You did blow up his tank,' said Benbow.

'Nobody treats me like that. I'll show Garracker who runs this City! Disowned me! Hah! We'll see.'

Benbow felt a hand on his shoulder. It was Wilf, watching Dowie with wide-eyed curiosity. Dowie didn't even spare him a glance, but broke into a run, heading down the street. Benbow felt Wilf's hand tighten.

'Benbow,' murmured Wilf, 'shall I go to Garracker, and tell him who I am?'

'Not now, Wilf. He's angry.'

'No, he's not.' Indeed, Garracker seemed to have already forgotten Dowie. He was giving directions to the men who had climbed down from the other cabs, and were now unloading rolls of wire, posts and toolboxes from the truck. Under Garracker's instructions, they began to hammer posts into the ground.

Some of the braver children edged closer. The men eyed them with distrust, and cast nervous glances at their dogs.

'I'm going to talk to Garracker,' said Wilf. His fist clenched and unclenched. Although Benbow could not smell his fear through the sharp yellow camouflage of his antiseptic, he knew he was afraid.

'No, Wilf!' he said emphatically.

'No, Wilf!' echoed Natty in alarm.

'Stay here, Wilf,' said Daffodil, with a shiver.

McCool strolled up, eased his shaggy back under

Wilf's hand, and leant against his leg. 'Do what you have to, Wilf,' he said. 'I'll come too.'

'All right,' said Wilf. With McCool beside him, he walked through the throng of City dogs, past the wary men, and up to Garracker.

Garracker took no more notice of him than Dowie had. He was busy trying to get something out of the back of the truck. Something that didn't want to come. Something hidden under the tarpaulin, that Garracker coaxed, and wheedled, and chanted to in a low, sing-song voice; and finally, climbed in after, and dragged out.

Slane.

Chapter Twenty-five

'Get that fence up!' roared Garracker at his workmen. '*Quickly*! What are you hanging around for?'

The men stopped gawping at Slane, and hastily began stretching wire netting between the posts. But Slane had no intention of trying to escape that way. He took one look at the mob of panting dogs and pointing children, and bolted, with high-pitched cries, in the opposite direction. Darting past statues, he disappeared from sight in the Museum's gloomy interior. Benbow heard his distant wailing, like a lost seagull.

'Don't follow!' Garracker shouted to his men, who looked relieved. Garracker himself ran after Slane, and Wilf ran after them both.

'Come back!' cried Natty. 'Oh, Benbow, we've got to stop him!'

They pushed through the crowd and into the Museum. Not far in, they found Slane crouching in a dark corner, rocking to and fro. Garracker knelt by him. When he reached out a hand, Slane spat, snapping his teeth, and lashed out with both arms.

Garracker sat back on his heels. There were shadows under his eyes.

'Can we help?' asked Benbow unwillingly.

'No,' muttered Garracker. 'He's already destroyed a whole floor of Prospect Towers. He won't understand me. He won't talk. I thought, just now and then, that... but it's no good. He can't speak. Breaks things. Won't eat anything but rat. Throws it around.'

Benbow studied Slane, who was beating his head against the wall behind him. Slane was clean, and well-dressed: his hair was neatly cut, except where a jagged slice implied that the barber had abandoned the job in a hurry.

'Thought he might be happier here,' said Garracker, who by contrast was unshaven and dishevelled. 'Thought he might be pining. Thought seeing his old haunts might help. Wonder where he slept. Slane. Slane boy.' He spoke in a quiet, exhausted monotone, which Slane ignored.

Wilf looked at them inscrutably with his one good eye. Then he squatted at Slane's other side.

'Go away,' said Garracker tiredly. But Slane, instead of spitting at Wilf, reached out a hand to touch his vivid hair. He made a noise in his throat.

'You like it?' asked Wilf. He carefully removed the wig, and held it out to Slane.

Slane took it slowly. He turned it over, sniffed and tasted it, then put it on his head.

'Hair,' said Wilf. 'Hair.'

Slane made a noise that wasn't hair, but wasn't entirely different. He widened his eyes and showed all his teeth.

'He likes it,' whispered Natty, in distress. Slane took the wig off, put it on Wilf's head, snatched it back and cuddled it.

'He should have a dog,' said Wilf. 'Cats aren't good for him.'

Garracker stared at Wilf. 'Do you know Slane?' he asked hoarsely.

Wilf hesitated. 'I did once.'

'I've seen you before. Who are you?'

'You've seen him at the Station,' Benbow supplied swiftly. 'He lives there.'

'That's it . . . ' Garracker frowned at the hair in Slane's hand. 'I'll buy you another wig. He's keeping this one.'

'All right,' said Wilf. But Natty tiptoed up and slipped a ragged woollen hat onto his naked head.

'Ay!' said Slane, pointing at the hat.

Wilf shook his head. 'No. Mine.' Slane accepted it, lost interest. Wilf took his limp hand. 'Sleep,' he said. Putting his head on one side, he closed his eye and let his mouth fall open. He snored. Slane cackled, then snored too.

'Sleep?' repeated Wilf. 'Where?' He pulled Slane to his feet.

'Look out!' cried Garracker. For Slane began to run with long, jerky strides, Wilf clinging to his arm.

'After him!' panted Garracker. Slane swerved round broken cabinets and pillars until he reached the remains of a staircase that climbed halfway to nowhere. Beneath it was a narrow alcove stuffed with rags. In a long, pitted stone trough, charred pages fluttered blackly.

'That's a coffin!' said Garracker, aghast.

'It's his fireplace,' said Wilf.

Fumbling in the rags, Slane pulled out a box of matches.

'No,' said Garracker. 'Give them here!'

But Slane had already struck one, and held it to the

paper in the coffin. He produced a book from under the rags and carefully tore out pages, feeding them to the fire. Then he sat back and stared at the flames. His face eased. His limbs relaxed, and he sighed.

'He likes the fire,' said Natty softly.

'Fire is his mother. It's his friend,' said Wilf, half to himself. 'It warms him. It plays with him. He needs fire.'

'He needs to be watched,' said Benbow.

'He will be. Fire and a watcher. He shall have them both, here in his home,' said Garracker, his voice ragged. 'I'll rebuild the Museum, clean it out, make it fit to live in. I'll build him a playground. And a schoolroom. I want him to speak. I'm going to employ special teachers. I've found one already – she said he should be in the company of children. Find me some children, Benbow.'

'They're not— ' started Benbow, but Wilf forestalled him.

'I could be one.'

'Yes. Yes, I want *you*. He likes *you*,' said Garracker. 'Find me some more. You can share his schooling. I'll build rooms for you too. I'll feed you, I'll clothe you, whatever you need. I'll get doctors in to keep him healthy, and you too, and the other children that you find for me. I want you to stay with Slane.'

Wilf gazed at Slane, gazing into the fire.

'He might like water,' said Wilf reflectively. 'He might like a pool, and a fountain.'

'We'll build it,' said Garracker. 'We'll pipe in clean water. Will you stay with him? I'm going to bring him toys, games. You can share those too.'

'Don't overdo them,' said Wilf. 'Not too many toys. Nothing noisy just yet. Get him a big quilt he can hide under. And balls and giant boxes he can play with. And a *dog*. He really does need a dog.'

Garracker glanced at Benbow. 'Perhaps one of—'

'No,' said Benbow.

'I'll find one,' said Wilf. 'I'll find one he'll like, who'll like him.'

'Yes,' said Garracker humbly. 'Will you stay with Slane? I want to hear him talk. I need to see him smile. Will you stay with him? Please. Whoever you are.'

'Oh, Wilf!' breathed Natty, stricken.

Wilf looked at her, and then at Garracker, and finally at Slane's blank, uncomprehending face.

'All right,' said Wilf. 'I'll stay.'

Chapter Twenty-six

Far out in the City, a pair of bloodhounds were barking faintly as they started on their night hunt. Inside the Station, Benbow had finished for the day.

He chewed on a mutton-bone, donated by Dowie, and probably stolen. For once, Benbow didn't care.

'That bone smells disgusting,' remarked Tonto. He looked longingly at Benbow's basket. 'You can share my last tin of Slinkypuss, if you let me sleep in your basket again.'

'No deal,' rumbled Benbow.

'Selfish mutt,' said Tonto. 'No offence.'

'None taken,' said Benbow contentedly. He gnawed the bone a little longer, then raised his head to ask Elise, who lay dozing by the stove, 'How long do you think it'll last?'

She opened her eyes. 'This peace? Garracker's good-will?' She yawned. 'Who can say?'

'I give it a month at most.'

A coal shifted, rustling, in the stove. 'I'm not so sure. It could last longer, if Slane doesn't break Garracker's heart . . . '

'Does he have one?'

'Oh yes,' said Elise. 'Everyone does. He's just discovered his. Must be a bit of a shock.' She stared into the fire; its coals glowed in her eyes. 'I think he loves Slane hopelessly, despairingly.'

'*Garracker?*'

'Who knows?' she mused. 'Because of Slane, he may come to value Wilf. Maybe learn that City children aren't disposable. Perhaps, in time, he may even accept Dowie.' Her head dropped back onto her paws.

Benbow was sceptical. Perhaps a new home in the City might be possible, after all, for Slane and Wilf and a few others, but he had no faith in Garracker's constancy. 'I don't see it,' he said.

Elise shrugged. 'Who can look into the future? We're all walking in the dark. You just do the best you can. Whatever happens, I won't be part of it.'

Benbow felt a chill run through his belly. 'Why? Where—'

'I'm retiring,' said Elise. 'I've got a place in kennels earmarked, by a farm, willow trees, a pond. No more City streets. You'll take over here, of course, Benbow.'

'Me?' said Benbow, shocked. 'No, I can't!'

'Why not?'

'Of course he can't,' sniffed Tonto. 'The service needs young blood. And a full complement of legs.'

'For once, he's right,' admitted Benbow. 'I could do it for a while, but in the long term the police need someone younger, fitter, to be in charge . . . '

'Like one of your clones?' Elise suggested.

'A clone?'

'Why not? You could run the Station to begin with, train him up in the meantime. In a couple of years, I think he'd make a good chief.'

Benbow's mouth fell open. Elise sounded as if she'd

worked it out long since.

'They're all good dogs,' he said, wondering, 'but which one do you—'

He was interrupted by doors banging loudly. Paws thudded up the stairs, and McCool, Araby and Daffodil burst in. With them was a small, clumsy mongrel with a spaniel's floppy ears and the alert eyes of a terrier. It fell over its own feet, got up and stared at Benbow's mutton bone as if trying to memorise it.

'This is Douglas,' said Wilf, coming in behind the dogs. 'I think he'll do for Slane.'

'He wants to be with a boy,' explained McCool, 'and he doesn't mind who.'

'He's not very clever, but he's quite sensible,' said Wilf. 'Doesn't scare easily. Hates cats.'

Douglas switched his attention to Tonto, and gazed at him with the same hungry concentration he'd given to the bone. Tonto bristled, and slunk out of the room.

'Carlo and Tomahawk are downstairs, eating all our bacon,' said Araby. 'Tomahawk's offered to be one of the children who'll live with Slane. Worth a try. She's tough enough. Slane won't be easy to live with.'

'He's not that bad,' said Wilf.

'What about Carlo?' asked Elise.

'If we can persuade him,' said Araby. 'He'll find it hard in the City, with that leg. But Garracker's getting a doctor in... I thought Carlo might go back to the Recycler, but he's too proud.'

'Anyway, she's got Nile now,' McCool added. 'Weird choice, but it seems to work. And it means there are no more Warriors. Since Nile left, they've all hung up their helmets.'

'So she's still the caretaker,' said Daffodil. 'I mean she's still taking care – I don't know what I mean.'

'I do,' said Araby. 'A child or two, for a year or two. She does what she can.'

'Hmph!' said Benbow. 'Wilf, why don't you show Douglas the kitchen and give him something to eat? You can take him to the Museum tomorrow.'

'We're going this evening,' said Wilf firmly. 'I promised Slane. Come on, Douglas! Natty's got some nice rat downstairs for you.'

Douglas lifted an ear – which promptly fell over one eye – and trotted out obediently after Wilf. The other dogs remained, flopping thankfully around the stove.

'Dowie's in a good mood again,' said Araby. 'I'm suspicious. I think he's planning ways to annoy Garracker. Or it might just be because he's started to grow beans on the Town Hall roof. I'm not sure, but I'll find out.'

Benbow looked at Elise.

'Araby,' he said. She nodded.

'What?' said Araby. 'I think he's got chickens too, only he's not letting on. Trugg told me – a load of squawking stupid birds, she said, taking up half the ballroom.'

'Angel's gone,' said McCool. 'Saw her crossing the northern Fringes, on her own. She looked happy.' McCool sounded wistful. 'How old do you have to be to train for undercover work?'

'One,' said Benbow. 'Not long now.'

Daffodil said, 'I'm worried about Natty.'

'Why?'

'She's pining for Wilf. She can see him slipping away and she doesn't want him to go.'

'Gotta take his own road,' said McCool.

'He's growing up,' said Elise, 'whether she likes it or not.'

'Things change,' said Benbow. 'All the time.'

'Yes, but what about Natty?' pleaded Daffodil.

'Lots of children in the City need looking after,' said Araby. 'She'll find another, or another will find her.'

'But it's Wilf she wants now!'

'Then you be her companion for a while,' said Benbow. 'Give her support. Make her feel needed. You're good at that, Daff.'

'Am I?' said Daffodil eagerly. 'Am I, actually?' His tail began to wag.

Araby looked at McCool and shook his head. 'How can he be our identical twin?'

'He's not,' said McCool. 'We're all just brothers. Shove over, bro, you're blocking the stove.'

The five dogs snuggled closer to each other and the fire, yawned and dozed.

'I expect it'll all be different tomorrow,' murmured Benbow to Elise's back. 'Something else will go wrong. The pigs will escape. Slane will flood the Museum with his new fountain. Dowie will try to blow up Prospect Towers . . . but I don't care.'

And he laid his head down by his plastic paw, and lulled by the breathing of his brothers by his side, and the distant barking of his cousins in the City, Benbow slept.